A COZY CAPE MAY AUTUMN

CLAUDIA VANCE

CHAPTER ONE

Dave and Margaret sat on the couch together and stared at the laptop screen feeling hopeful and excited.

"Well, should I click confirm?" Margaret asked after a deep breath.

Dave leaned forward and put his arm around Margaret's shoulders while staring at the screen. "Definitely. Let's do it."

Margaret clicked, waited for the confirmation to pop up, then closed her laptop and let out a loud squeal. "Oh my gosh. I'm so excited!"

Dave leaned back on the couch and let out a loud sigh. "You're telling me. I can't believe we're really doing it."

Margaret sat back and nuzzled her face in Dave's flannel shirt while wrapping her arms around him. "I simply cannot wait. I'm bursting at the seams right now."

Dave hugged Margaret tight. "Me too. By the way, what time did you say check-in is tomorrow?"

Margaret paused for a moment. "The Black Horse Inn's website says you can check in at 3 p.m. My gosh, there's so much we have to do before then."

Dave gently pushed a strand of hair out of Margaret's face. "Are you sure staying in Cape May is what you want to do?"

Margaret picked up the steaming cup of cinnamon apple tea off the coffee table and let the mug warm her hands before taking a satisfying gulp. "Definitely. I can't wait to cozy up to my man at a fancy B&B during autumn in Cape May without any work obligations to deal with. It's been a dream of mine since we started dating, actually."

Dave smiled. "Really? You're making me blush."

Margaret took another long sip of her tea and set her mug down before glancing back over at Dave. "There's just something about autumn and being in love. The crisp, cool nights. The campfires. The snuggly sweaters. The soft flannels. The hot drinks that warm your whole body after a sip. I could go on forever. Don't get me started. But really, getting to experience all of that with *you* is the icing on the cake."

Dave reached over to Margaret's hand and rubbed it. "Well, when you put it that way, it makes Cape May seem like the best possible place for us to relax and unwind after a pretty busy year. Have we really not taken any time off together since we became a couple?"

Margaret thought for a moment. "Nope. I just rolled my vacation days over at Pinetree Wildlife Refuge and with the B&B, it has been hard to get away."

Dave nodded. "Yeah, I did the same over at Pinetree. Well, I'm glad we're finally taking some time for us. It's past due, and this is a nice start."

Margaret pulled the throw blanket off the back of the couch and snuggled into it. "It really is getting chilly lately. Didn't we just have the air conditioning on last week? I'm this close to putting the heat on, but I won't."

Dave laughed and looked at Margaret's colorful fuzzy socks peeking out from under the blanket before noticing Harper and Abby walk into the room. "Hey, you two."

Harper and Abby nestled onto the couch between the happy couple and got under the blanket with Margaret. "Can we go to that Ghoul Spring Village thing? A lot of our friends at school are going," Harper asked.

Dave furrowed his brow. "Oh, isn't that something they do over at Historic Cold Spring Village? It's like a haunted walk amongst the old historic village? I've heard it's pretty neat."

Abby raised her hand in the air to get Dave's attention. "Yes! Can we go?"

Margaret half-seriously hemmed and hawed. "I don't know. It might be too scary for you two."

Harper rolled her eyes, almost looking like the teenager. "Mom. It's not too scary. I heard little kids go to it, and we're *not* little."

Dave nodded. "She has a point there, Margaret. They're practically teenagers at this point," he said jokingly, as the girls were still in elementary school.

Margaret bit her lip. "Well, I guess it would be nice and festive to go, especially since we might not see you two until after our vacation. Are you all packed to stay at grandma and grandpa's like I asked?"

Abby nodded excitedly. "Yes! I can't wait. Grandma said we're going to bake all kinds of things together, and they're taking us to some Halloween events too."

Dave laughed. "Gee, I thought you two might be a little sad that we're going off to spend time together for a while, but clearly you both have your own fun plans lined up."

Margaret shook her head and laughed. "I can't keep up with their social lives."

Harper jumped off the couch. "Well, you better let Aunt Liz and Uncle Greg know that we're going tonight because Michael and Steven told me they're going. Let's all meet up."

Margaret smiled. "You bet. Now, go layer up. It's dropping into the fifties tonight."

Dave looked back over at Margaret wrapped up tight like a burrito under the blanket and chuckled. "So, everything is set for us? There's really not much else we need to do?"

Margaret nodded. "We just have to show up. It's all handled."

Dave leaned over and kissed Margaret on the head. "It's going to be perfect."

* * *

Just after sunset, Dave pulled his truck into the Ghoul Spring Village parking lot with the girls and Margaret.

"Well, this place is hopping. You all ready for some ghostly ghouls and creatures of the night?" Dave asked, holding his hands out like claws.

Harper laughed. "Yes, we are! Oh look, there's Michael and Steven. Let's catch up to them."

Margaret looked through the front window, caught Liz's eye, and waved. "They see us. They'll wait. No need to rush."

It was too late. The girls hopped out of the truck and headed over to their older cousins, whom they loved to see.

Margaret and Dave followed behind, hand in hand, smiling as they eyed where everyone was congregating.

Liz and Greg gave a hug to Margaret and Dave before Liz saw someone in the parking lot walking over. "Over here, Sarah! Chris, Sam!"

Margaret whipped her head around. "Well, you didn't tell me they were coming too! How nice."

Liz smiled. "Totally last minute, but I think Donna and Dale are stopping over as well. Oh, wait. I think I see them now."

The next thing they knew, they had themselves a nice big group to walk through the haunted village with. The friends strolled the eerie path, so rich with history and decorated for the spooky season at the same time. They stopped at the Cold Spring Country Store first, which was decorated with cobwebs and orange and purple Halloween lights. Outside by the front step stood a woman dressed in black with lit candelabras on her table.

Harper and Abby walked up to the lady's table to get a closer look with Michael, Steven, and Sam. "Well, this is neat, but why is it called the haunted walk?" Harper asked suspiciously.

Michael shrugged while Steven and Sam went back on the path. "Beats me," Michael said.

"Come on, girls. Let's keep walking," Margaret said as she waved them over.

Suddenly, the group found themselves encompassed by a large hazy fog. Walking a little ways through it, when it finally dissipated, they saw gravestones lit by red uplights and an old-style chopping block.

Margaret watched as the girls tiptoed around the lingering fog, angling for a closer look at the gravestones. When a masked individual dressed as a monster appeared near them, Abby yelled, "I'm out!" as she ran back over to the adults, who all put in a valiant effort to hold in their laughter.

Harper looked back at Abby. "Abby, it's fake. Look, it's not real. You're not really a monster, are you?" Harper asked as she stood before the scary costumed person. The monster looked at Harper and shrugged, not sure how to answer the brave little girl.

Dave took Margaret's hand in his again, and Margaret's heart leaped as she looked at all of the colorful foliage in the trees above them and smelled the campfires that burned in the distance.

Dave pointed ahead at the low-lying natural fog around the village. "I'm pretty sure that's not from the fog machine. Nature is helping with the spookiness tonight, that's for sure."

A pirate ship with skeletons aboard was lit up with red lights in the dark of the night. Unafraid, Harper walked right up to it and peered inside. When the spooky captain wearing a big red hat popped up directly in front of her, he nearly scared her half to death. She let loose a bloodcurdling scream before booking it back to the adults who stood watching.

Dave laughed. "They finally got you, Harper! I witnessed it. You were scared."

Harper turned red, feeling defeated but excited from the adrenaline at the same time.

They made their way to the end of the haunted path and stopped to talk while the kids grabbed some Halloween treats from the long candy chute.

"Hey, everyone!" Margaret yelled to get the group's attention over the different conversations happening among them.

"I just want to make sure you got my email about dinner on the thirtieth? Dave and I thought it would be nice to end our local vacation with a scrumptious meal with friends and family."

Sarah nodded. "Oh, that's right. I forgot to respond. We'll be there."

Everyone else gave an affirmative response to going, which made Dave squeeze Margaret's hand a little tighter.

Donna reached into her purse and held up a handful of tickets. "Hey, guys. A friend of the family is running a hayride at a farm on the outskirts of Cape May. They gave my parents a bunch of tickets. Anyone up for going?"

Everyone looked around at each other, nodding.

"Sounds great. It's still early in the evening, I say let's do it," Liz said while looking at the group for reassurance.

Dave glanced at his truck. "Well, guess we'll meet you all over there? I've got some blankets in my truck for the hayride. It may get a little chilly."

Twenty minutes later, they drove down a long winding gravel driveway onto the farm's property. Rows of dried cornstalks lined either side of the drive, and a few people in reflective security vests and light up batons motioned where to park in a big grassy field.

Donna led the group when everyone reconvened after

getting out of their cars. Under the bright moon, she looked ahead at the roped-off area near the ticket booth and turned around. "Well, it looks like we missed the line. I don't see any. I'll hand out everyone's tickets now so we can hop right on."

Sure enough, by some miracle, they'd missed the crowd and were able to get on the hayride as soon as they walked over to the tractor that already had people on it waiting to go. Margaret and Dave squished in together on the hay bales, while the kids all sat together across from them, and Liz made a point to sit next to her sister.

Just as the tractor started up and got moving, Liz turned to Margaret. "This might not be the best place to have a conversation, but I'm curious, did you see Dolly's email this afternoon?"

Margaret looked back at Liz with a surprised face. "No, I haven't checked my email since this morning. What did she say?"

Just then, an enormous animatronic spider appeared next to them, popping out from behind a tree. The entire group screamed, then laughed after realizing what it was.

Liz looked back at Margaret after clenching Greg's arm with a death grip. "Well, she and Kim are ready to come back. She insinuated that they'd like to return to their old hours."

Margaret watched as the tractor pulled through a dark tunnel with floating candles along the sides. A mad scientist cackled as he experimented with gooey green bubbling potions.

"Well, how is that going to work? We hired Irene, Jackie, and Bonnie during their extended time off. We can't just take away their hours to give back to Dolly and Kim, can we?" Margaret asked as she grabbed Dave's arm when they started approaching another dark tunnel.

It was pitch-black and terrifying, but that didn't stop Liz from continuing the conversation. "Well, no, I don't think we should do that. It wouldn't be fair. Obviously, we can have Dolly and Kim there on the days we don't have anybody, but maybe they can also work *with* Irene, Bonnie, and Jackie. What do you think?" Liz asked as she ducked to avoid the flying monkeys above them.

They finally got out of the tunnel where Margaret had a second to respond without interruption.

"Can we afford that? We'd be paying five people to work at once, when we really only need two to three. Dolly and Kim prefer to work together, but so do Irene, Jackie, and Bonnie. We can't divide them up," Margaret said as she quickly buried her head into Dave's jacket as a masked man jumped onto the hayride with a chain saw.

Liz screamed and squished her whole body into Margaret and Dave while grasping onto Greg as the chain saw (without the chain) came closer. All of the kids screamed and ran to squeeze in between them.

Dave laughed at Greg who was being used as a human body shield. "I think she's offering you up to the chain saw guy," Dave said trying to catch his breath between laughs.

Greg laughed and rolled his eyes. "I see how much my wife loves me right now."

After the chain saw debacle, everyone caught their breath, including Liz who had hay stuck all over her knit sweater and hair. "This is what I'm thinking," she said as she plucked some pieces of straw out of Greg's jacket. "We'll have them work together, even if we're paying more people than we need to. Just think of all of the time it will free up for us. I think the more, the merrier. I bet it will work out perfectly. Not to mention I'm exhausted always juggling so many things at once between jobs, my kids, my house, my husband—"

"Hey, I heard that," Greg said with a chuckle.

A large vampire creature popped out from the bushes, scaring Donna and Sarah half to death as they screamed then burst out laughing.

Margaret sighed, then tapped Liz on the shoulder. "Look. I agree about being exhausted. Maybe it'll be worth it to have them all work together. I'm sure they'll get along great too. They seem somewhat similar. They're around the same age and have similar interests."

Liz laughed. "Similar interests? Like what? Running a B&B?"

Margaret shrugged her shoulders. "Well, yeah."

Just as the hayride came to an abrupt stop, Liz glanced back at Margaret. "OK, good. I'm glad you're on board, seeing as they are starting back to work tomorrow. I kind of told them they could have their hours back already." Liz winced slightly at her sister. "I knew you'd be away this week, and I thought the timing worked out perfectly. You'll be able to enjoy your vacation fully knowing the Seahorse is in good hands. I hope that's alright."

Margaret laughed while Dave helped her down the stairs off the hayride. "So, you asked me all of that while vampires were popping out, and you had already told Dolly and Kim that they could have their hours back? What am I going to do with you, sister?"

Liz shrugged and smiled. "You're going to come hang out with me more with all of your new free time, that's what."

CHAPTER TWO

The next afternoon, Dave pulled his truck up to a dark-green Victorian with black shutters in Cape May, fully decorated for autumn and Halloween with pumpkins of all sizes and colors leading up the brick front steps.

"Is this the one?" Dave asked, feeling unsure.

Margaret looked at the sign hanging off to the side. "It says *Black Horse Inn*. So, yep, this is it."

Dave rubbed his chin, noticing an elderly lady siting in all black on the front porch rocking chair staring straight at them. "How exactly did you find this place again?"

Margaret glanced at the black wrought iron fence that surrounded the entire bed-and-breakfast and the four humongous old oak trees that lined the street in front of it. "Well, it was literally one of the few bed-and-breakfasts that weren't booked up. I imagine this is somewhat of a busy week for visitors who want to come see Cape May in it's peak autumn glory, and we waited very last minute to find something, remember?"

Dave nodded as he found a parking spot, then hopped out to grab their suitcases before heading to the front steps.

"Oh, hello there," Margaret said as she took notice of the old woman in the rocking chair.

The woman kept rocking while staring straight at them with a stone-cold expression.

Dave shifted his eyes, uncomfortable with the strangeness of the woman. Carrying on, they entered through the front door into a somewhat dark and quiet establishment. "Hello! Anybody around?"

Margaret peeked her head into the dining room, looking for someone who worked there. "Are they open?"

"Welcome. You must be Dave and Margaret?" a voice said from upstairs.

Margaret looked over to see a pale woman in her sixties with extra-long silver hair and deep-brown eyes approach.

"That would be us," Margaret said as she glanced over at Dave with a smile.

"Well, I'm Anne, and I run the Black Horse Inn. Let me show you to your room. I think you'll … quite enjoy it," she said as she led the way up the creaky steps.

Dave walked behind Margaret and Anne, holding the luggage and feeling an oddness about the place. "So, Anne. The place been busy?" he asked as he looked around the empty inn.

Anne laughed. "You can say that. You're the first to check in, but we're booked solid this week. All ten of the rooms, that is."

Margaret nodded, feeling relief that they wouldn't be the only ones staying at the B&B. "Well, that's great to hear."

As they got to the third floor, Anne took out a key, opened a door, and stepped to the side to allow Margaret and Dave to walk through. "Here we are. The honeymoon suite. Our most prized room. It really is … something," Anne said as she gazed around the large room with adoration.

Margaret furrowed her brow. "Oh, there must be a

mistake. We aren't on our honeymoon. We aren't even married yet."

Anne ignored Margaret and walked into the room with them. "Did you see the wood-burning fireplace? There're fresh-cut logs beside it for you to use. We just ask that you follow all of the safety measures listed in our guest book on the nightstand. I'll let you two get settled in. Give a bloodcurdling scream if you need anything," Anne said with a laugh as she disappeared out of the room.

Margaret gave a little chuckle, then set her purse down on a small chair by the door and proceeded to walk around the room as Dave stepped into the bathroom. "Did you see this huge four-poster bed with the canopy, Dave?"

Dave mumbled something incoherent from the bathroom as Margaret continued to explore the room.

"This fireplace is dreamy. I can't wait to cozy up next to it, and—wow, look at this view out the window," Margaret said excitedly as she looked out onto the shady, tree-lined street just as a trolley and horse carriage passed by.

Dave emerged from the bathroom, then eyed the floral wallpaper all over the room. "Well, it certainly has that old Victorian charm, I guess."

"What? You don't like it?" Margaret asked as she flopped onto the bed that held more pillows than necessary.

"I didn't say that," Dave said as he wiped some dust off the mantel above the fireplace with his finger, then studied it. "It's just old, and well, it's missing some of the amenities I'm used to when staying at hotels. Like a TV."

Margaret shrugged. "Well, I can see that, but I think it will make us go out and do things more instead of holing up in this room."

Dave sat next to Margaret, then tickled her. "What's wrong with holing up with each other while we're here? You, me, Anne … that old scary woman on the rocker. We'll have a ball!"

Margaret laughed until tears rolled out of her eyes at Dave's absurdity. Finally composing herself, she said, "Oh, I forgot to tell you. We have dinner reservations at Panico's at five, but first, maybe we can walk around the neighborhood."

* * *

Across town, at the Seahorse Inn, Dolly and Kim were back on the job after taking a long break to be with family. Arriving to meet Irene, Bonnie, and Jackie for the first time, Dolly opened the door to the Seahorse and took notice of all the autumn and Halloween decorations that weren't there the last time they'd seen it. "What in the world is all of this?"

Kim stepped inside behind Dolly and eyed the place up along with her. "Looks like they did some heavy decorating. I like it. It's festive."

Dolly shook her head. "It's gaudy. That's what it is. A little something is fine. This is an all-out Halloween store in here. I'm waiting for a zombie to pop out of the closet."

"Jackie," a woman called as she descended the stairs holding a tote full of cleaning supplies. "I finished cleaning the rooms. They should be ready for our check-ins at four."

"OK!" Jackie yelled from another upstairs room.

Taking notice of Dolly and Kim, she smiled. "Hi, there. Welcome to the Seahorse—"

Dolly cut her off with a sharp laugh. "We're not here to check in. We work here. I'm Dolly. This is Kim. We haven't met you yet, I don't believe."

Reaching the bottom of the steps, she set her tote down and stretched out her gloved hand towards them. "I'm Irene."

Dolly glanced at the blue kitchen glove that went straight up to her elbow before Irene noticed.

With a chuckle, Irene pulled off her glove and extended her hand once more. "Let's try this again without my cleaning gloves. I'm Irene."

Dolly and Kim both shook hands with her before glancing around the heavily decorated foyer again.

"Oh, the decorations. They're something, eh?" Irene said.

Kim smiled. "They sure are."

Dolly rolled her eyes. "Yeah, something is right."

Just then, Bonnie walked out of the kitchen with an apron on and hand towel on her shoulder. "Irene, I think we're set for teatime. The cheese and fruit trays are prepared. We just have to put it out when it's that hour. Oh! Hi there," Bonnie said taking notice of Dolly and Kim.

Dolly furrowed her brow. "Hi. Did you say cheese tray … for teatime?

Bonnie shifted her eyes around the room. "Well, yes, I did."

Dolly set her bag down with force, then marched into the kitchen with everyone following behind her. "Cheese trays are for the wine hour not teatime. When on earth did this start happening?"

Bonnie, still not sure who Dolly was or what was happening, widened her eyes at Irene. "Um … who are they?"

Dolly sighed, overhearing Bonnie's question to Irene. "I'm Dolly and this is Kim. We ran this inn for Margaret and Liz before taking a little sabbatical before *you all* were hired."

Bonnie nodded, still unsure of what was going on. "OK …."

Dolly looked around the room in a huff. Noticing the kitchen table was pushed too close to the island, she proceeded to move the entire thing back with her brute force. "We leave for over a month, and it's like all chaos broke loose. What is going on here?"

Kim shrugged as she glanced over at Irene and Bonnie, feeling slightly embarrassed.

Dolly walked to the refrigerator and whipped the door open before laughing loudly. "Just when I thought things couldn't get worse, they have. Who on earth thought to chill the red wine for wine hour? Only the white wine should be here," she said as she pulled the bottles out one by one.

Bonnie stumbled on her words. "Well, I … didn't put them in there."

Kim piped up, trying to smooth out the situation. "Dolly, I'm sure they got put in there by accident. Everything is fine. Let's not step on these fine ladies' toes. They're doing a good job."

Dolly spun around and put her hand on her hip. "Kim, you'd better put your bag down. We have our work cut out for us this evening."

Kim made a hesitant laugh. "OK then."

"What did I miss?" Jackie asked as she appeared, holding a basket with the dirty linens.

Irene and Bonnie widened their eyes and glanced at Jackie. "Dolly and Kim are back. That's what."

* * *

Meanwhile, in West Cape May, Liz was at home in overalls, a bandana wrapped around her head, paint splattered all over her.

She ran to the fridge, pulled out her water bottle, and chugged it while eighties top hits blared. She wiped her mouth with the back of her arm before walking back into the living room and picking the paint roller back up. She rolled the dark forest-green paint up and down the wall, making sure to be as perfect as possible.

After getting half a wall done, Liz stepped back, and glanced around the living room. Tarps with fresh paint drips were strewn around the furniture and floors when Greg walked in from running errands. "Whoa. What is going on here?" he asked.

Liz yelled over the music. "My client canceled on me. I

have the next two weeks free. So, I decided to finally do all the projects that I haven't had time for."

Greg turned down the music. "Well … OK, but I kind of liked the eggshell walls we already had in here. They brightened the room up. You know, made it look larger."

Liz shook her head, then pointed at the green paint on the one wall. "We need something bold. Something that makes a statement. I'm kind of sick of the crisp, clean, boring look of our home, honestly."

Greg folded his arms and looked at the mess of a living room, then at the crown molding trim around the windows, door frames, and lining the top of the walls. "OK, well what are you thinking for the trim? Keeping the classic white, I hope?"

Liz moved to the side to get a wider angle look of the room. "Nope. The trim will be the same color as the walls. You have to trust me on this."

Greg sighed. "Fine, I'll trust you. I guess I have to. Anyway, it's only one room. I can live with that."

Liz shifted her eyes. "Actually, I'm doing the dining room, as well. I also have some new light fixtures and furniture that will be arriving. I hope you don't mind that I made all these decisions without you?"

Greg shook his head. "Well … I have to say that I kind of *do* mind. I live here too."

Liz latched onto Greg's arm. "I wouldn't have done this if I didn't think you'd like it too. I just knew that if we got into a discussion about it, that my vision would never happen as I see it in my head. What I'm doing is something I've been doing for clients all year, and they absolutely love it. Obviously, I hire painters to do my clients' homes instead."

Greg took another deep sigh. "Just please leave the comfy sectional couch. I will not be happy if that's replaced with some tiny trendy uncomfortable one."

Liz laughed. "Definitely, hon. I wouldn't do that to you.

Though, I've always wanted to try my hand at sanding and refinishing hardwood floors. That may be something on my radar with this ...."

* * *

Dave and Margaret walked up the steps of the old blue church that had been converted into Panico's, an Italian restaurant in West Cape May.

"Hi. We have a five o'clock reservation for Margaret. Party of two," Margaret said to the hostess as they walked inside.

"Perfect. Your table is ready. Follow me this way, please."

Once they were seated, Margaret and Dave glanced over at a savory pizza coming out of the brick oven. Before they could say anything, another couple around their age was seated directly next to them.

Dave happily nodded hello to the couple before perusing the menu. "Do you want to split an appetizer?"

Margaret smiled. "Yes, but there's so much to choose from. What do you think about the bruschetta or the burrata?"

Dave read the bruschetta description aloud. "Thin focaccia, chopped tomato, onion, basil, parsley, fresh mozzarella, balsamic glaze, baked. Well, I'm sold."

The woman from the couple sitting next to them cleared her throat. "Sorry, I couldn't help but overhear your conversation. I just want to say that we ate here last night, and that bruschetta was amazing. I recommend it."

Margaret smiled. "Well, then, we're definitely getting it. Thank you."

Just then, their server came to the table. "Hi! I'm Cassie. I'll be taking care of you tonight. Can I start you two off with any drinks?"

Dave's eyes widened as he reached below his chair, pulling out a chilled bottle of sauvignon blanc. "I almost forgot I brought this. Also, we'll take two glasses of water, please."

The server reached into her pocket, pulled out a cork screw, uncorked the bottle of wine and poured it into their long-stemmed wine glasses. "There you are."

Margaret took a sip of her wine. "Oh, it's perfect. Cassie, we'd also like the bruschetta as an appetizer."

"Great. I'll put that in now and come back in a bit to get your entree orders," Cassie said as she hurried off.

Dave took a sip of his wine, then scanned the room, taking in the warm, inviting ambiance of the restaurant before stopping to gaze at the fired-up brick oven full of pizzas.

The woman next to them noticed where Dave was looking. "Have you had the pizzas here? They're really good. We had one last year around this time."

Dave shook his head. "I haven't, but they do look fabulous."

The woman's husband spoke up. "Where are our manners. I'm Ernesto, and this is Shannon. Since we're practically eating dinner together, we might as well introduce ourselves," he said with a chuckle.

Dave stuck his hand out for a handshake. "Nice to meet you. I'm Dave, and …"

Margaret chuckled. "And I'm Margaret. Are you two visiting Cape May?"

Shannon took a sip of her ice water. "We are. We live near Philadelphia. We love coming to Cape May in the autumn when the leaves are changing and the Victorians feel even older and spookier. We're actually doing a stop-and-go trolley tour of haunted places in Cape May."

Margaret's eyes widened. "You are? Oh, that sounds fun. We're from Cape May, but haven't done any of the ghost tours. I guess we thought it was for the tourists and not us locals."

Shannon glanced around the room, as though to make sure no one else was listening, then looked back at Margaret and Dave. "Our friends stayed at one of the bed-and-breakfasts on

18

the tour, and they told us some pretty strange things happened. I mean *really* strange."

Dave laughed. "Well, I don't know how real these haunted tours are. I think it's just a bunch of made-up ghost stories."

Ernesto shook his head. "I don't know about that. Our friends have made us believers."

Shannon piped in. "We actually have two extra tickets for tomorrow night. Our friends had to cancel last minute. Would you two want to join us?"

Margaret's eyes lit up. "That actually sounds amazing. What do you think, Dave?"

Dave shook his head, then chuckled. "Well, I guess we're going then."

CHAPTER THREE

The following afternoon, Dave and Margaret walked hand in hand around Washington Street Mall, which had a variety of restaurants chock-full of people eating their lunches outside in the crisp autumn weather. Then, there were the busy retail shops and of course all the other people enjoying a nice relaxing walk, taking it all in, just like Margaret and Dave.

Margaret stopped at a Cape May sign hanging at the top of an arbor in the middle of the pathway. It had cornstalks on either side tied in the middle with big orange bows and below it, multiple hay bales and pumpkins. She smiled to herself at the people walking by holding hot beverages and bundled up in sweaters.

"This is pure bliss. Why don't we vacation more often in our own hometown?" Margaret asked Dave.

Dave laughed, then shrugged. "I mean, this is quite relaxing. Do you want to peruse some stores?"

Margaret nodded and pointed towards Whale's Tale, a well-loved gift shop that had just about everything. "How about we go there first?"

They walked into Whale's Tale and were immediately overcome by all of the colors and delightful items around them.

Everything from candles, seasonal napkins, books about Cape May, cards, and toys surrounded them.

Margaret stood before an autumn-themed section with festively designed plates, mugs, napkins, and soaps. She held up a pack of napkins decorated with black cats, pumpkins, and colorful leaves and studied it, feeling the softness of the napkins and the crinkle of the plastic packaging on her fingers.

"What do you think, Dave? Will these work for our *special* dinner with friends and family?" Margaret asked as she displayed the napkins to him.

Dave smiled. "I like them. If you think so, I say get them."

Margaret did a giddy hop before grabbing a handful of the napkin packs.

Dave paid at the register, and then halfway down the block, Dave stopped dead in his tracks. "You know, there's this book I've been meaning to get. Would you mind stopping in at the Cape May Bookstore?"

Margaret looked down the strip. "Oh, the Cape Atlantic Book Company. Yes, let's do it!"

They got to the building that housed the bookstore, and took the escalator upstairs to where it was located. Dave made a beeline to one end of the bookstore while Margaret browsed the different shelves, not really looking for anything in particular.

Something caught her eye, and she stopped to pick the book up. "*Spooky Cape May Stories.* Huh," she said as she flipped through the pages.

Dave came around the corner holding his book. "I found it. I've been looking for this book for a while. It's the history of North Cape May. Since I bought my home there, I've been wanting to know more about it."

Margaret smiled. "Oh, I love that. Look what I found, a book of Cape May ghost stories. I think I need this."

Dave rolled his eyes and chuckled. "Whatever makes you happy. How about we pay and go grab lunch. I'm famished. I was thinking maybe The Ugly Mug? I haven't been there in a while. I could go for a nice burger, and it's the perfect day to eat outside. What do you say?"

Margaret nodded. "Definitely. I'm also starving, and I could go for some of their clam chowder and a salad."

After paying, they headed over to The Ugly Mug, and luckily were able to grab the last outdoor table available under the awning. They ordered and Margaret promptly took her new book out of the paper bag, set it on the table, and glanced through each individual story before stopping at one.

"You've got to be kidding me. The Black Horse Inn is in here. There's a whole ghost story about the place."

Dave crinkled his brow. "*Our* Black Horse Inn? The one we're staying at?"

Margaret's eyes widened. "Yes! Oh, this is both exciting and eerie. I can't wait to dive into this story."

Just then, their server arrived with Margaret's soup. "Here you are, miss. Would you like some oyster crackers?"

Margaret quickly put her book away, then smiled at the server. "Yes, please."

Dave chuckled as he watched Margaret place her head over the steamy soup, letting herself inhale the savory aromas. "Well, are you going to eat that or give yourself a steam facial?"

Margaret laughed but not before glancing down at her book in its bag on the ground, feeling excitement, happiness, and intrigue overcome at her all at once.

* * *

As Donna flipped through the clothing racks at a thrift shop a couple of towns over, her eyes lit up. She pulled a purple linen tunic off the rack, noticing that it was an expensive brand that would surely net her a nice profit online. She studied the shirt, looking for any flaws, when her eyes were drawn to a small hole on the back.

"Ugh," Donna blurted out as she hung the tunic back on the rack. When her phone rang from her purse, she plucked it out and answered it. "Hey."

"Hey, what are you up to?" Dale asked cheerfully.

Donna sighed, still quickly flipping through the clothing racks with her free hand. "Just trying to find items to resell from the thrift store. It's not going too well."

Dale frowned. "Sorry to hear it. Why is that?"

Donna picked up another shirt, noticing a large yellow stain on the front, and promptly put it back. "For the past couple of weeks, I haven't found much to sell. It's like these thrift stores have all dried up. I don't know what I'm going to do. I think it's time for me to rethink my career choice. Actually, I did start looking up courses on becoming a teacher. I'm starting to think I should get the ball rolling with that. They wouldn't start until January, though."

Dale's eyes widened. "Well, that's great that you're thinking ahead to the future. Have you thought about substitute teaching at some of the schools around here? It might be good practice for you, and you'll get paid. It may alleviate some of this thrifting stress that you're experiencing."

Donna paused and bit her lip in thought. "You know, that thought never even crossed my mind. I'll look into it later today. Thanks, Dale."

"No problem," Dale said, feeling satisfied with himself.

Donna sighed. "I haven't even asked how you were. I'm sorry, Dale. It's just this stress I'm having right now."

Dale smiled. "I'm great, and I totally understand. I've been there with my businesses. Self-employment can be very stressful. There's no guaranteed income like there is when you have a stable nine-to-five. I'll let you finishing thrifting, I have to get to the restaurant. Call me later."

Donna said goodbye, then put her phone back in her purse, all the while feeling defeated and hopeful at the same time.

* * *

The sun had set, and since Chris was working, Sarah opted to spend time with Chris's son, Sam. He was eight years old, and though it had been over six months since she and Chris had started dating, she'd never had one-on-one time with Sam.

Sarah pulled her car into Dawson's Farm's parking lot. Dried cornfields, laughing families, and light beams from flashlights were all around them.

As Sam and Sarah got out of the car, she noticed that darkness had spread throughout the sky, so she put her hand on Sam's back to lead him to the corn maze.

"You have the flashlights?" Sarah asked.

Sam nodded and proceeded to stop and open his backpack, taking two large flashlights out. Handing one to Sarah, he said, "Here you go. I've never done a flashlight corn maze before. This should be fun."

Sarah nodded, then turned her flashlight on and shone it towards the maze. "Well, I guess we give them our tickets at the entrance. Let's head over."

As they walked toward the entrance, Sam's eyes widened. "Oh my gosh! There's my friends! I can't believe it! Brandon! Terrance! Billy! Over here! Over here!"

Sarah smiled at him while handing their tickets to an employee. "That's great. Do you want to go over and say hi?"

Sam hopped up and down with excitement. "Yes! But they just went into the maze. We have to hurry and catch up with them."

"OK. We will. Give me a second while I tie my shoe," Sarah said as she kneeled down. Instead of waiting, Sam bolted into the dark corn maze and out of sight. When Sarah looked up from tying her shoe and realized Sam wasn't with her anymore, she began to panic. "Sam? Sam! Where are you?!" she yelled.

Other parents and kids walked by her, not really sure of what to make of all her yelling. With no time to spare, Sarah turned on her flashlight, and made her way into the corn maze, walking at a fast pace to try and catch up with Sam.

He must have been very far ahead because it didn't matter how fast she walked, she couldn't find him. Her heart raced each time she caught up to other groups of people only to be met with a dead end over and over again.

She finally stopped walking and took a breath to compose herself, when a familiar voice came from behind her. "Sarah?"

Sarah whipped her head around, the sound of someone she knew almost making her heart skip two beats.

"Judy! And Bob, Harper, and Abby. Boy, am I glad to see you all," Sarah said feeling relief and anxiety simultaneously.

Harper looked around the dark corn maze with her flashlight. "Are you here by yourself?"

Sarah shook her head and took a deep breath. "No, I'm with Sam … or *was* with Sam. He kind of jetted off with his friends, and I've been trying to catch up with him for twenty minutes. I'm going to lose it in a minute."

Bob chuckled. "I've been there. We've had many incidents with the girls running off at carnivals when they were kids. Do you remember that, hon?"

Judy shook her head. "Don't remind me. I thought I was going to have a heart attack."

Abby shone her flashlight straight ahead, and straightened herself out. "I've done this corn maze before. I know my way around. Follow me, and we'll find Sam."

The adults all nodded at each other, impressed with the stand-up leadership that Abby exuded. Sure enough, their group followed her right out of the flashlight-lit corn maze all the way to the end.

Sarah took a look around, noticing all of the firepits and

vendors dishing out hot apple ciders before her eyes landed on a gaggle of kids roasting s'mores over a firepit off to the side, Sam smack in the middle. "There he is!"

"Now that you've found him, we're going to grab hot cider with the girls, Sarah. We'll catch up later," Judy said as she ushered the girls to the drink stand.

Sarah nodded before staring back at the group of kids. "Samuel! Get over here!" she yelled at the top of her lungs, adrenaline coursing through her veins.

Sam froze while roasting his marshmallow and widened his eyes. Sarah guessed he realized that he probably was in trouble as he watched her stomp over to him.

"Sam, where did you go? You can't just run off like that. I was worried sick! You could have been kidnapped or hurt. How could I have known?"

Sam's friends quietly chuckled, while Sam sat on the bench and stared at his feet. "You're not my mom, OK? I thought we were here to have fun. I didn't know I had to be chained to you."

Sarah was taken aback. She had never heard Sam talk like that to his father or his mother or … anyone. "Sam, I know I'm not your mom. We did come here to have fun, but you're still a kid. It's unsafe for you to run off like that."

Sam looked over at his friends' parents, who were off congregating by the food stands, then back at Sarah. "I want to leave."

Sarah took a deep breath, trying to compose herself. It was the first time that she had an opportunity to bond with Chris's son, and it was an absolute disaster. She felt horrible looking at how sad Sam suddenly appeared. Playing the scenario back in her head, she wasn't sure if she'd overreacted or not.

* * *

Across town, Dave and Margaret boarded the Cape May Ghost Tour trolley with Shannon and Ernesto.

Shannon was bursting with excitement. "I can't wait for this! I seriously can't believe you live here and have never done this. I'd do it twice a week, if I could."

Dave laughed. "I think once will be enough for me."

Ernesto nudged Dave. "Shannon got me into this. I was just like you, then bam! I'm all intrigued by this ghost stuff now. It gets you, I tell ya."

Dave chuckled with skepticism. "Yeah, we'll see about that."

Margaret shook her head and giggled. Dave was doing something so far out of his element, but the fact that he did it for her made her heart nearly leap out of her chest.

A middle-aged gentleman wearing a black top hat and monocle cleared his throat at the front of the trolley and spoke into his microphone. "OK, everyone. I'm Stan, your guide. Find your seat so we can start the haunted tour. There's so much to talk about and see. Wouldn't want you to miss any of it."

Dave laughed at the absurdity of the situation and grabbed Margaret's hand. "Are you ready?"

Shannon, who sat in front of them with Ernesto, whipped around to face Margaret and Dave. "By the way, this new ghost tour also stops at the locations and lets you walk around and possibly go inside."

Margaret smiled, then looked out the trolley window as it started to move. "How exciting. Thank you again for giving us your extra tickets."

Stan began the first ghost story as they stopped at an extravagantly large blue mansion that was completely dark except for the old lampposts near the front steps. Everyone disembarked from the trolley and stood on the sidewalk facing the front of the house.

"This here is the Bluebird Mansion. It was built in the late

1800s and there have been reports from the past owners of paranormal activity—drawers opening and shutting, the living room TV being turned to the same station every morning before anyone was awake, and doors opening that were completely shut. Around 1960, a fire destroyed half of the house. It was rebuilt to what it is today and has changed ownership four times. The current owners have said that a bouncing ball sometimes appears for no reason," Stan said as he looked around the group.

Margaret nudged Dave. "A bouncing ball?"

Dave shrugged. "Like the kind out of a gumball machine?"

Shannon chimed in, while grasping Ernesto's arm. "I'm betting it's the bigger kind. You know, like the ones kids play with on the playground? Almost like kickball size …."

Stan pointed to the house next door. "Now, let's all head next door to the North Star Bed-and-Breakfast."

Margaret and Dave started to walk, but were stopped when Shannon grabbed their arms. "Wait. I need to see this ball," she whispered. "Let's walk around to the back door and peek in."

Dave shook his head. "I don't know about this. Do the owners really want us looking through their windows and doors?"

Ernesto glanced at the house. "There's nobody there unless they like sitting in the dark."

Shannon grabbed Margaret's hand, and they giggled as they discreetly walked to the back door.

Dave sighed. "Well, I guess we can't just stand here, Ernesto."

Ernesto nodded. "Yep. Let's go make sure they're not getting into trouble."

When they all got to the back door, which had a large unblocked window to peer through, they stared into the house.

"What are we looking for exactly?" Margaret asked as she looked inside.

Suddenly a red ball came bouncing down the stairs, proceeding to roll straight towards them and stopping in front of the door.

Shannon screamed and ran towards the street. "That's it. I'm out of here."

Ernesto followed behind her. "Wait for me, hon."

Dave and Margaret stood there with their mouths gaping open, still processing what they saw.

"I'm sure someone is home and tossed that ball down the steps," Dave said as he started walking away.

Margaret turned to follow him, but not before taking one last peek at the ball and wondering if this was all part of the tour.

CHAPTER FOUR

Margaret and Dave walked onto a farm late the next morning, wondering exactly what they signed up for.

"Hey folks! You here to see the alpacas?" a man asked as he headed towards them.

Margaret nodded and held up her tickets. "Yep. I bought tickets for the eleven o'clock alpaca tour."

Dave smiled and looked around. "Can't say I've ever been up close with an alpaca before."

The man chuckled. "You've come to the right place. This here is my alpaca farm. Well, mine and my wife's, I should say. Wouldn't want to anger the missus. Lord knows she's the boss around here," he said with a loud laugh. "Anyhoo, the rest of the group got here early, so if you want to head on over with me, we'll start the tour shortly."

Margaret and Dave followed the quirky man to a fenced-in area where about ten other people stood looking at the furry creatures.

"Howdy, folks. Allow me to introduce myself. I'm Fred, and these alpacas you've come to see are my life. We started this farm twenty years ago, and they are our doll babies, even ole Gertie over there, who hates everyone including myself," Fred said with a chuckle as he pointed to the disgruntled looking black alpaca laying on the ground.

"Anyway, I have baggies of cut-up carrots to feed them, if you'd like, while I go over some interesting tidbits on alpacas," Fred said as he handed out the carrots.

After Dave and Margaret grabbed their alpaca treats, they walked over to the fence line with everyone else and proceeded to feed the animals.

Fred cleared his throat. "Some quick alpaca facts before we delve more into the information. Did you know that alpacas are considered clean animals? They rarely ever smell bad. As a matter of fact ..."

While Fred continued to talk, Margaret walked over to Gertie, who was being ignored by everyone. She put a carrot stick through the fence. "Here ole girl. Wanna carrot?"

Gertie looked at Margaret and her carrot, snorted and rolled her head back.

Margaret laughed. "Yep. I guess she hates me."

Dave smiled, then stuck his carrot through the fence. "Here, let me try."

Gertie stared at Dave for a few seconds, then proceeded to get herself off the ground and slowly walk towards Dave.

Margaret's eyes widened. "Whoa. What's going on here?"

As Gertie got closer to the fence, she stuck her head over it, while gently smelling Dave's jacket and then finally nuzzling her face all over it while making a clucking sound. Margaret smiled and held her hand over heart at how endearing the whole thing was to watch.

Fred who still jabbered on, stopped mid-sentence when he saw Gertie loving on Dave. "Well, I'll be. In the fifteen years we've had Gertie, I've never seen nothing like this. Everyone take a look at this milestone moment of Gertie being affectionate."

Dave stood laughing and smiling as Gertie rubbed her

head on him, completely ignoring the carrot sticks that he still held onto.

Fred chuckled. "Sir. Not sure if you and your lady are married, but I'm pretty sure Gertie wouldn't be opposed to a date."

Margaret laughed at both the cuteness and absurdity of the situation. "Dave, we may have to come visit Gertie more often, especially if you're the only person in the world she likes."

Dave smiled and shrugged. "What can I say? I'm irresistible, I guess."

* * *

Harper and Abby walked into their grandparents' home after being picked up from school by Bob.

"Hi, Grandma!" Abby and Harper yelled in unison as they dropped their backpacks on the couch.

Judy smiled while picking up the backpacks and putting them by the coat rack. "Are you two hungry? I'm making chicken pot pie tonight."

Harper scrunched her nose. "A chicken pie? Gross."

Bob chuckled. "You mean to tell me you've never had a chicken pot pie? It's quite delicious. Piping hot cut-up chicken with vegetables baked in a flaky crust. Yum," he said as he rubbed his stomach.

Abby nodded. "That sounds good and all, but we really want to go pick apples. We heard some kids at school talk about it."

Bob looked at his watch. "Well, dinner is not for another two and a half hours, right, dear? Maybe we can fit that in."

Harper and Abby squealed in excitement. "Yay!"

Judy sighed. "Shouldn't they be doing homework or something? Is there really time for this?"

Bob waved his hand dismissively. "They can do it after

dinner. Come on, it'll be fun. When's the last time you went apple picking?"

Judy thought for a moment, then shrugged. "I can't even remember. When I was a kid?"

Bob nodded, feeling satisfied with himself. "OK, kids. Let's go now so there's time to get everything else done later."

Twenty minutes later, they had pulled into the farm market, and were walking towards the apple orchards.

Bob got to the apple picking stand, and handed over his credit card. "We have four for apple picking today."

The woman smiled. "Would you like to walk to the orchards or take the hayride to them? It's an extra five dollars per person. It should be back within five minutes to pick the next round of people up."

The girls' eyes widened. "Can we do the hayride? Please, please, please!" Abby begged.

Judy looked at Bob. "Gee, I don't know … we're on a time constraint with dinner and homework."

Bob shrugged. "Let's just do the hayride. The girls seem excited."

Judy looked at her watch. "Well, OK, but then we have to go straight home. I still need time to prepare dinner before we eat."

The girls high-fived just as the tractor pulled up and the people got off with their full bags of apples.

They embarked the hayride once it was clear, and eventually were off to do some apple picking.

Thirty minutes, and four huge bags of gala, honeycrisp, and jonah gold apples later, they were back from apple picking and walking towards the car, when four kids crossed their path carrying large pumpkins to a covered area with picnic tables.

Abby stopped dead in her tracks. "Where are they going?"

Judy squinted her eyes to get a better look. "Oh, it looks like there's some kind of pumpkin painting class going on. Unfortunately, we have to get home."

Harper stood next to Abby, unmoving, as Judy and Bob tried to persuade them to the car.

"Come on, girls. We have dinner to eat, homework to do— not to mention bedtime, which isn't too far away," Judy said as she waved them towards the car.

Abby stuck out her bottom lip and crossed her arms. "I'm not even hungry. Why can't we stay here?"

Harper pointed to the painting class. "Look, I bet if we ask, we might be able to do a quick painting on a pumpkin. I'm sure we'll still have time to do everything else."

Judy shook her head. "Girls, it's not going to work. Trust me."

Harper and Abby then looked at Bob. "Grandpa. What do you think?"

Bob, caught off guard, hemmed and hawed. "Well, your grandma makes the rules."

Tears welled up in Abby's eyes, and the next thing they knew, they were all sitting at a picnic table painting pumpkins. After lots of fun painting pumpkins, the sky had turned completely dark, and they finally walked back to the car.

Judy looked at her watch. "This can't be right. Is it really eight?"

Bob glanced at his phone. "Um … that's correct. Oh boy," Bob said as panic started to set in.

Judy shook her head. "Not only do we not have time to make dinner, but the girls will only have a half-hour to do homework before bedtime. We're getting fast-food for dinner. It's the only thing there's time for."

The idea of fast-food for dinner excited the girls more than anything as Margaret rarely ever let them eat it.

However, while the girls were excited, Bob and Judy were suddenly wondering who exactly was calling the shots anymore between the kids and adults.

* * *

Liz stared at the empty freshly painted green living room and blew a stray hair out of her eyes before starting up her electric hardwood floor sander that she'd rented.

When she'd started sanding, she heard a phone ring. She stopped and pulled her phone out of her pocket. It wasn't hers. She looked around the downstairs until she finally saw Greg's phone sitting on the kitchen island.

"You left your phone at home again, Greg," Liz said while rolling her eyes and walking towards the phone. She had dropped his phone off at the restaurant more times than she could count.

Liz picked the phone up and stared at the name, trying to figure out who Katie was. Was there a Katie that worked at the restaurant? Not that she knew of. Maybe a family member? Nope. Suddenly Liz's chest felt heavy as her mind jumped to the worst.

Liz thought of calling the first person she wanted to talk to, but thought better of it. "Margaret is on vacation. I'm not bothering her with this," Liz said out loud.

The next thing she knew, she was dialing Sarah's number.

"Hey, Liz!" Sarah said, as sounds from the busy coffee-house could be heard in the background.

Liz composed herself and put on a smile. "Hey, Sarah. So, I was just calling because … well, are you busy?"

Sarah loudly threw something in the garbage. "Well, sort of, but I can talk. What's up?"

Liz swallowed hard. "I think I just need someone to talk to right now. Greg left his phone at the house, and someone named Katie just called him. I can't think of any Katies that I know. I guess my mind is just thinking the worst, and I need someone to talk me out of it."

Sarah chuckled. "Just ask him when he gets home. I'm sure it's nothing. Plus, men who cheat aren't going to put the woman's actual name in their phone, right?"

Liz laughed. "You know, you're right. Plus, Greg wouldn't

cheat. I can't believe my mind even went there. I'm sorry. Now I feel stupid for calling."

Sarah smiled. "It's no problem at all. You still doing home projects over there?"

Liz sighed while glancing at the dusty mess on the hard-wood floors. "Yep. I'm too far in to stop now."

"Well, swing by here if you need a break. Coffee's on me," Sarah said as she put the last chocolate croissant into the pastry display.

Liz breathed a sigh of relief, and hung up with Sarah, ready to start sanding the floors again, when she heard a ding. Greg had a received a text message.

She stared at his phone that was still in her hand. It was Katie again.

Hey. So, what time do you want meet today?

* * *

That evening, Margaret and Dave participated in the special evening hours at the Cape May Lighthouse. Climbing up the 199 steps of the spiral staircase to the top, Margaret stopped halfway and caught her breath. "Phew. I think I'm really out of shape because this is not as easy as I remember."

Dave chuckled from behind her. "Well, I bet the view will be worth it. I've never done this at night."

When they reached the barred-in deck area at the top, a handful of people were already up there, and Margaret imme-diately smiled and inhaled the crisp autumn air deeply. Ahead of them was the full moon, casting a glow right onto the World War II bunker on the beach in the distance.

"Wow," Dave said as he wrapped his arms around her from behind. "This is something. Being up here at night is so ..."

"Romantic?" Margaret said as she looked up at the sky.

"You could say that. I guess the bright moon is drowning

out the stars, but this is something," Dave said as he gave Margaret a squeeze.

A chilly breeze swept in, causing Margaret to shiver. "It's dropping down to the forties tonight. It's going to be a cold one."

Dave smiled. "Should I finally get a fire going in our fireplace at the B&B? Seems like the perfect night for it."

Margaret felt her body warm at the thought of it. "That actually sounds perfect."

Forty-five minutes later, they were back in the honeymoon suite at the Black Horse Inn with Dave having already successfully started a fire in the fireplace. Margaret poured two glasses of red while Dave grabbed some pillows off the bed and created a comfy cozy sitting area near the fire.

Margaret handed Dave his wine, and they sat on the floor next to the crackling embers. She stared at the orange flames, drawn in by how relaxing and mesmerizing they were.

Dave took a sip of his wine, then looked at Margaret. "So, we're all set for everything on the thirtieth? Did everyone respond?"

Margaret nodded. "Yep. Everyone's coming to the dinner. Your family, my family. Our friends. I can't wait."

Suddenly, a loud bang sounded over their heads.

"What was *that*?" Margaret asked while staring at the ceiling.

Dave shrugged. "Probably just the people staying on the floor above us, I'm sure. Maybe they dropped something."

Margaret shook her head. "It sounded like they dropped a bowling ball. Not to mention … aren't we on the top floor?"

Dave thought for a moment. "You know, we are. I guess that's the attic above us. Maybe it's the owner looking around."

Margaret stood up and walked to the door. "I'm going to peek my head out. I'm curious." Upon opening the door, Margaret gasped loudly. Staring straight at her—close enough that they were almost nose to nose—was the old woman in black from the porch.

Anne swooped in and put her arm around the old woman's shoulders, ushering her down the steps. "I'm so sorry. I hope we didn't disturb you."

Margaret worked on catching her breath as she shut the door and sat next to Dave.

Dave chuckled. "You think she wanted to play Scrabble?"

CHAPTER FIVE

"These don't go here," Dolly said as she moved the clustered rocking chairs apart on the front porch of the Seahorse.

Kim sighed. "Well, I didn't do it."

Dolly shook her head. "Kim, I know you didn't do it. It's *obvious* who did."

Kim rolled her eyes, then proceeded to help Dolly space the rocking chairs back out.

"There," Dolly said as she placed the last chair in the perfect spot.

Kim chuckled. "Well, I'm glad it's to your liking now. We wouldn't want the guests to be too close together now would we?"

Dolly squinted her eyes. "Very funny. I'm going inside to start cleaning. Lord knows this place needs it. I saw dust caked all over the mantel."

Kim shook her head and muttered under her breath as she followed Dolly inside. "A little dust on the mantel, and now this place is a pigsty, apparently."

Dolly forcefully pulled the vacuum cleaner out of the hallway closet, plugged it in, and began vacuuming the rugs.

Kim hollered over the loud vacuum. "I'm going to go do laundry."

"What?!" Dolly yelled over the noise.

Kim pointed downstairs and yelled. "The laundry."

"The baby?" Dolly yelled back, confused.

"I'm going to do the laundry," Kim shouted just as Dolly turned off the vacuum.

Dolly held her ears. "OK, but did you have to holler?"

Kim shook her head and headed down the basement steps.

Dolly, feeling overly frustrated, realized the cord to the vacuum was about a foot too short to reach the entire dining room. She grasped the cord, trying to tug it out of the outlet, when *pop*! The electric went out.

A few minutes later, Kim stood in the darkness of the basement trying to feel her way around.

"Dolly!" Kim yelled.

Suddenly, footsteps could be heard coming down the basement steps.

"Is that you, Dolly? I can't see a thing. They have these thick curtains on the windows down here," Kim said as she tried to carefully find her way around.

"It's me. I think I blew a fuse when I pulled the vacuum cord out of the wall. Just let me find the breaker box. Ah! There it is," Dolly said as she used her phone's flashlight to locate the correct circuit to turn it back on.

"We have light again. Yay," Kim said unenthusiastically as the bulb hanging over the washer came on.

Upstairs, the front door opened, and they heard Irene, Bonnie, and Jackie coming in.

Dolly looked at Kim and sighed. "Well, at least we're only working an hour with them today."

Kim put her hand on her hip. "Dolly. Give them a chance."

Dolly crossed her arms. "Look. I'll give them a chance, but I don't like some know-it-alls coming in here and changing a perfectly good operation. We had this place running like a well-oiled machine, and now it's— I mean, there's dust on the mantel, and the front porch was a mess, and those rugs looked like they haven't been cleaned in a month. Is that what we want for our guests?"

Suddenly, Irene, Jackie, and Bonnie all walked down the basement steps.

"Oh, there you two are. We were wondering," Irene said happily.

Dolly looked at Kim, who in turn gave her a stern look. "Yes, here we are. Just getting some laundry done."

Jackie clapped her hands. "Perfect. Well then, I'll start putting fresh linens on the beds."

* * *

Donna smiled and placed a hand on her heart as she walked around the bright-yellow house right off the beach in Cape May Point.

"Hi, Lenore. Yes, I can show you the property in Frog Hollow," Derek, the realtor, said as he glanced at Donna. "Give me half an hour."

Donna felt her heart burst as she walked around the adorable sunny home, making sure to inspect every closet.

The realtor slid the phone into his pocket and walked over to Donna. "What do you think?"

Donna closed the closet door and looked over at Derek. "This is literally a dream. How many more people are you showing this to today?"

Derek nodded. "Well, you're the first person to ask for a showing. It was minutes after I posted the listing. Do you get email notifications or something?"

Donna shrugged. "Nope. I just happened to look right at that moment."

Derek smiled. "Well, I know the owner wants a background

check and credit report. If you're interested, I'll let him know you were the first, and I'll put in a good word for you. I think he's even interested in a rent-to-own option if that makes this place any more appealing to you."

Donna nodded. "Definitely. This is my dream home. Where do I send my information?" she asked as she glanced out the window towards the ocean.

Derek pulled a packet out of his clipboard. "Fill this out, and follow the instructions for the credit and background checks. You can leave the paperwork at my office tomorrow. It should only take a day or two for the owner to get the reports. I think I'm going to lock up now, if you want to take one last quick look. I've got to get to the other side of town."

Donna stood next to the butcher-block counter, running her hand over the smooth multicolored wood, then happily sighed. "I'm going to try and not get excited yet, but I have a really good feeling about this. I'm newly divorced and just moved back from California to start over. I've been at my parents' for months now. It's time."

Derek tossed his keys up in the air and caught them. "I'm going to send you all of the good luck. My advice to you is fill those forms out as soon as possible and add any other information you think will help the owner make his decision. You know, something like what you just told me," he said with a wink.

* * *

Before dinner, Margaret was itching to go to the West End Garage on Perry Street. It was a large building made up of over fifty different vendors selling a variety of items. They browsed the many different booths, stopping to look at some vintage collectibles and antiques.

Margaret held up a vintage white ceramic cat with blue rhinestone eyes. "What do you think? I love it."

Dave smiled. "I love its mid-century look. Do you want it? I'll buy it."

Margaret smiled. "You don't have to."

Dave playfully nudged her. "I know that. I *want* to. This is a special week, and I want you to enjoy yourself."

They meandered along until they came to another booth full of everything from candles to teapots to used books.

Dave's eyes widened as he kneeled down and pulled something stacked under the table. "Well, I'll be. If this isn't a sign, I don't know what is."

Margaret held her hand over her mouth and laughed. "Really? A used Scrabble game?"

Dave opened it up. "Well, let's hope all the pieces are in here because I think it's meant for us."

As they walked around the remaining booths, glancing at beautiful artwork and boutique clothing, they finally ended up by the register, where one last thing caught Margaret's eye—a rack full of beautifully packaged garden seeds. She rushed over, scanning all of the seeds before picking out a bunch of her favorites.

Dave waited in line at the register and looked over at her just as he was about to get rung up. "What do you have there?"

Margaret smiled and brought the seeds over. "They have the silver leaf sunflower seeds I've been looking all over for. Not to mention these heirloom tomatoes that I can't wait to try."

Dave smiled and nodded at the woman ringing them up. "We're getting these as well. It looks like we're garden planning for next year already."

Margaret nudged him. "It's never too early to plan for the future."

Dave nodded. "Or too late for that matter."

* * *

Chris got behind the wheel of his pontoon boat while Sarah untied the boat from the dock.

"OK, we're good," Sarah said with a thumbs-up to Chris, who nodded and steered the boat into the inlet towards the bay.

Sarah stood next to Chris at the wheel. "How's business been now that it's colder?"

Chris bobbed his head side to side. "Well, it's definitely nothing like the summer, but we have our regulars that come on the weekends. They enjoy being out on the boat."

Sarah dug her hands into her hoodie's pockets. "So, I've been meaning to talk to you about something."

Chris looked over at her with anticipation in his eyes. "OK, shoot."

Sarah deeply sighed. "Well, you know how it was just Sam and I the other night? And how we went out together?"

Chris nodded. "Yeah, you went to the corn maze, right? Did everything go OK?"

Sarah shrugged. "That's the thing. I don't think so. He ran off with his friends, and I couldn't find him for like a half hour. When I finally did find him, I let my temper get the best of me, and let's just say, I think he hates me now."

Chris slowed the boat to a stop along some marshy grasses, then deeply sighed while looking out towards some shorebirds off in the distance. "Yeah, about that …"

Sarah felt her stomach flip with anxiety. "About what?"

Chris shook his head. "I think Sam is acting up because he's having a hard time with the divorce lately."

Sarah furrowed her brow. "But the divorce was five years ago."

Chris shrugged, not sure of what to say. "I guess now that he's older, he sees it in a different perspective. Then again, I've noticed it more since his mother got a new boyfriend."

Sarah's eyes widened. "Does he not like the boyfriend?"

"I'm not sure. I've never asked him. I guess I should find out," Chris said as he stood and took the wheel again.

Sarah thought for a moment, remembering when her parents split when she was six years old. Her father married rather quickly to an evil-spirited woman who only looked at Sarah as a hindrance to her marriage with her father. It tore her up.

"Chris, stop the boat," Sarah said as she took his arm.

Chris pulled the boat off to the side. "What's going on?"

Sarah shook her head. "I think we need to have a talk with Sam together the next time he's over. I want to make sure he's not going through what I did when my parent's split. It took years of therapy in my twenties to finally move past it. It was awful."

Chris pulled Sarah in for a tight embrace as the pontoon bobbed in the wake of a passing boat. "How come you never told me?"

Sarah looked away from Chris out the window, while brushing a tear out of her eye. "Trust me, I haven't told many people about it. It's not something I want to remember, let alone discuss any further. It practically destroyed my relationship with my father."

Chris pulled her in tighter as she buried her face into his jacket. "We will definitely talk to Sam. As for you, I want you to be able to talk to me about anything," he gently put his finger under her chin and lifted her face to his. "You know that, right? That you can talk to me about anything?"

Sarah nodded and wiped her last tear out of her eye with her sleeve. "I do."

* * *

Dave and Margaret were seated for dinner at Tisha's outside patio. Margaret sipped her glass of chardonnay and released a satisfying sigh as she took in all of the colorful foliage around them.

Dave, engrossed in the menu, took one last look and set it down on the table. "I know what I'm getting."

Margaret picked up her menu. "I haven't even looked yet. I'm too busy admiring everything around us. What are you getting?"

Dave lifted the menu up again and glanced at it. "The seafood risotto, of course. I get it every time."

Margaret chuckled. "Don't you want to try something different for once?"

Dave smiled. "I can try some of yours."

Margaret giggled and shook her head. "Well, I'm getting the harvest salad. It sounds perfect for autumn. Baby greens, roasted butternut squash, blue cheese, green apples, candied pecans ... and a balsamic vinaigrette to finish it off."

Dave nodded. "That sounds good. Maybe I'll get that before my meal."

Just then, Margaret's eyes widened. "Oh my gosh! They have stuffed pumpkin gnocchi in a sage brown butter. That will be my entree for sure."

The waiter came by and took their orders, leaving them holding one hand across the table while sipping their wine.

"So, last night was kind of crazy, right?" Margaret asked as she leaned forward with excitement and intrigue.

Dave laughed. "Oh yeah. The old woman at our door. What was up with that? Do we even know her name?"

Margaret shook her head and thought for a second. "Wait a minute. Remember when we checked in, the B&B owner, Anne, said that they were completely booked? I'm now realizing we haven't seen or heard any other guests."

Dave scratched his chin. "I thought that's because we're always out doing things. We barely spend time there except to sleep. We haven't even tried their breakfast yet that comes with the room."

Margaret laughed. "That's mostly because we've been waking up late and missing it."

Dave nodded. "That's right. Who knew we could sleep so late?"

Margaret smiled. "I think my body needed it. I've never felt more refreshed."

After their meal, and a little dessert and coffee, they headed out for a walk down Lafayette Street.

Dave pointed towards Rotary Park. "They're watching a movie in the park, look at that."

Margaret's eyes widened. "Oh my gosh. I bet it's a Halloween movie. Look at all those kiddos."

Dave nodded. "And plenty of adults. You wanna go check it out?"

Margaret put her arm through Dave's as they walked over and found a grassy spot to sit. Most of the other people there had blankets and chairs and even movie snacks.

Dave subtly grabbed Margaret's hand and put it up to his lips and kissed it. "I'm glad I'm going to be spending the rest of my life with you."

CHAPTER SIX

Bright and early the next day, Margaret and Dave awoke and made their way to Poverty Beach.

Dave yawned, then unfolded their towel and spread it over the sand. "Come, sit with me," he said to Margaret.

Margaret smiled and moved right next to him so they were touching. "So, we're watching the sunrise. Didn't think this would be on our agenda," she said with a giggle.

Dave rubbed his eyes. "Me neither, but I think we'll be glad we did."

Margaret nodded. "Not sure how you got me out of that warm bed. It was pretty rough."

Dave shook his head and smiled while watching the sun crest over the horizon, illuminating the water and sand in the process.

Margaret leaned her head onto his shoulder and took a deep breath. "This is just so refreshing. We're already up and have the whole day to do what we want. What shall we do next?"

Dave turned to look behind him. "I know a place we can go."

They walked across the street to a coffeeshop and ordered a couple of coffees to go before strolling down the promenade.

Dave stopped in front of the arcade and took a long sip of his coffee, then turned to Margaret with a mischievous smile. "Wanna play skee-ball?"

Margaret nodded and laughed. "Sure."

Dave stopped her at the entrance as they walked in. "I'm warning you. I'm really good at this. I've won a championship or two."

Margaret rolled her eyes. "A skee-ball championship? In what world?"

Dave cracked his knuckles. "In this world, baby. Well, maybe it was the '80s world, but still. I was *the one* to beat. Picture this— me, fourteen years old, surrounded by tons of kids, and every fifty- or hundred-pointer I got, the place erupted. I felt like a rock star."

Margaret laughed. "So, you're telling me that I'm marrying a skee-ball champion and didn't even know it?"

Dave smiled as they walked over to the multiple rows of skee-ball and put quarters in the slots. "Maybe. Here, let's give it a shot. I'm probably quite rusty now."

Margaret rolled her eyes, then shuttled her ball up the ramp. She scored a fifty-pointer right away while Dave got a ten-pointer.

Dave glanced over, competitiveness roiled up inside of him. "OK. OK. I see what you did there. Getting your practice in."

Margaret narrowed her eyes at Dave before winding her arm up and rolling the ball right into the hundred-pointer, which was pretty tough to get. "How do you like them apples?"

Dave looked over at his measly twenty-pointer and shrugged. "It's a good start."

Margaret put her hand on her hip and stared Dave down. "OK, mister. We're going to have a good ole competition on these next games. Best out of five games, wins. You and me. Let's see if the *skee-ball champion* is still all that."

Dave wiped some sweat off his brow, turned his hat backwards and took off his flannel, exposing his short-sleeved shirt underneath. "You're on … but you're going down, sorry to tell ya," he said with smile.

Margaret did a couple stretches and jumped up and down a few times, as though she were a boxer loosening up. She placed her quarter into the slot, prompting the wooden balls to come barreling down the chute, loudly hitting each other in the process.

Dave shook his head and laughed. "Stretching for skee-ball. That's a first," he said as he wound up his arm and rolled his first ball of the competition.

Five games later, they compared scores.

Margaret scratched her chin. "Wow. Do you see what I see, Dave? I believe that I, Margaret Wilder, am now the new skee-ball champion."

Dave shook his head and chuckled. "OK, OK. I'll give you that win. You earned it."

Margaret grabbed his hat and put it on backwards before putting her cross-body purse back on and walking towards the exit. Abruptly, she stopped and turned to look at Dave with a smile. "I guess never told you. My uncle used to own an arcade in Wildwood, and we literally spent our summers playing skee-ball. For hours, and I mean hours. Just so you know that I wasn't exactly easy competition."

Dave nodded and smiled, feeling more attracted to Margaret than he'd ever been.

Hand in hand, they walked slowly down the promenade, taking time to let the world around them soak in, when a couple walking by stopped abruptly to do a double take.

"Margaret and Dave?"

"Shannon and Ernesto!" Margaret said happily. "You two are still here?"

Shannon nodded. "Oh, we definitely are still here. We

extended our stay because this place is wild, I tell ya," she said with electricity in her eyes.

Ernesto shook Dave's hand. "You wouldn't believe the things we've seen since we saw you guys. You think that ball bouncing down the steps of that old place was creepy, well we saw something even crazier."

Shannon leaned in, excitement bursting with every breath. "Come for a walk with us tonight. We're going back to Hughes Street. There's so much ghostly activity over there. It's insane!"

Dave furrowed his brow. "Wait a minute. What exactly did you see?" he asked with some skepticism.

Ernesto chuckled. "Oh, she won't tell you. She did this to me. She went for a walk, came back to our B&B in hysterics, but wouldn't tell me a *thing.* I had to put my shoes on in the middle of the night and follow her out there."

Shannon nodded enthusiastically. "So, meet us tonight. Say around nine?"

Margaret looked at Dave, who shrugged, not really buying any of it, but was somewhat intrigued to go along for the fun of it. "OK, we'll see you two there."

Shannon jumped almost three feet in the air while clapping her hands. "Oh, this is going to be so good. So good."

* * *

Hard rock blared as Liz (wearing her paint-splashed overalls and a bandana on her head) stained the newly sanded hard-wood floors in the living room and dining room a deep brown color. A song came on that hit at just the right moment, and Liz wailed along with the angsty song.

Greg came in from work, walked up behind Liz, and wrapped his arms around her. "Hey."

Liz whipped around to face him, dodging his kiss.

"What was that for?" Greg asked.

Liz shrugged. "What was what for?"

51

"That! You always give me a kiss hello," Greg said feeling a little confused.

Liz bit her lip, not sure if now was the right time to bring up what she saw on his phone. "I don't know. I have paint all over my face. I'm sweaty and gross."

Greg chuckled and tried to plant another kiss on her. "I really don't care about that."

Liz ducked from him and walked away. "So, the boys. Are they still at practice?"

Greg scratched his chin. "Yeah. They're getting dropped off by the Johnson's."

Liz turned the radio down before facing Greg. "Well, then maybe now is good to time to discuss this."

"Discuss what?" Greg asked perplexed.

Liz put her had on her hip. "Oh, I don't know. Discuss how your get-together with Katie was the other day, maybe?"

Greg shifted his eyes, nervousness setting in. "What are you talking about?"

Liz walked towards him, stomping her feet. "Don't play dumb. You left your phone here, and I saw you get a call from her and a text. I saw it with my own eyes. Who is she?"

Greg fumbled on his words, not exactly sure of what to say. "She's … helping me pick out new place settings for the restaurant."

Liz nodded angrily. "I'm not buying that, Greg."

Greg clenched his jaw, aggravation taking over him. "Look, Liz. Trust me when I say that nothing is going on, but at the same time I can't tell you why I met up with her."

Liz laughed sarcastically. "Can't tell me? Me, your wife. You can't tell *me*."

Greg nodded. "I promised a close friend I wouldn't tell. Just trust me on this."

Liz shook her head while staring at Greg. Then she stalked over to the speakers and turned the music up even louder than before. "Fine. Well, I'm getting back to work. You're on your own for dinner."

* * *

Judy had just pulled a pot roast out of the oven when Bob walked in from the backyard. His eyes widened. "It smells amazing in here, hon. I have a couple more things to do outside. What time is dinner?"

Judy looked at the clock on the wall. "Thanks, dear. Oh, give it about ten minutes. I need to let the roast rest before we cut it."

Bob nodded and walked out the back door to the yard.

Judy glanced at the girls slumped on the couch watching TV. "Girls! Come in here and set the table, please. We're going to eat shortly."

Harper and Abby glanced over, started to get up, but then stopped when their show came back on after a commercial.

Judy looked around the room. "Girls? Did you hear me? Can you set the table for me?"

Abby peeked over the couch. "It's getting to the good part. Can you give us five minutes?"

Judy put her hand on her hip. "Well, by then dinner will be ready. How about you can listen to it while you set the table?"

When Judy was met with silence, she grew impatient and set the table herself, then let everyone know it was time eat. That got the girls' attention, and they got up and sat themselves at the table.

Bob's mouth watered as he came back in and dished up Harper's and Abby's plates before placing them in front of each girl. "Here you go. This is one of your grandmother's specialties."

The girls looked unimpressed. Harper stabbed a carrot on her plate, then took a tiny bite before setting her fork down.

Judy finished chewing, and took notice of the girls barely eating. "What? You don't like it?"

Abby moved a piece of the roast around her plate. "Well, not really. Mom never makes this kind of stuff."

Bob took a sip of his iced tea. "What does your Mom normally make for dinner?"

Abby shrugged. "Noodles with cheese and peas. Or sometimes her and Dave make tacos. Some other stuff too."

Harper nodded as she sat back and folded her arms while staring at the plate.

Judy looked at the pot roast. "Well, what's wrong with this?"

Harper looked around the room. "I don't know. It looks weird. Can we get fast-food again?"

Judy shook her head, thoroughly aggravated. "Fast-food? Heavens no. This is better than any of that and healthier too."

After ten more minutes of watching the girls shove their food around their plates, not eating anything, Bob had had enough. "I'm going out to get them fast-food. They need to eat, and clearly they aren't."

Harper and Abby's eyes lit up. "Really? I want chicken nuggets and fries," Harper said.

"Me too," Abby said as she stood up from the table and put her plate full of food on the counter.

Judy rolled her eyes and glanced at Bob. "Fine, but this is the last time we're getting them junk."

After Bob picked up the chicken nuggets with fries and the girls ate, Judy stepped outside to call Liz.

"Hi, Mom," Liz said as she moved furniture around, still feeling frustrated from her conversation with Greg.

"Hey, Liz. You still doing your home projects?"

Liz looked at the half-stained living room floor. "You could say that. What's up?"

Judy lowered her voice. "I'm having a little issue with

Harper and Abby. I didn't want to call and bother Margaret on her vacation, so I'm calling you."

That got Liz's attention, as she stopped moving furniture to listen. "What's up?"

Judy sighed. "I think they're becoming a bit spoiled by us, and it's backfiring. We treated them to fast-food the other day when we were running late and didn't have time to make dinner, and tonight they wouldn't eat the beautiful pot roast I cooked because they wanted chicken nuggets and fries again."

Liz laughed. "Oh, geez. Well, what did you do?"

Judy rolled her eyes. "Your father went and bought them what they wanted."

Liz put her hand on hip. "Mom. You can't cave that easily. Stick to your guns. Also, your pot roast is good, but not all kids like that, and those two are picky eaters. Maybe ask them what they would like you to cook next time."

Judy paused. "You're right. I'll do that … although did I mention that they ignored me when I asked them to set the table?"

Liz laughed. "Mom, it sounds like you're being too much of a friend to them, and not enough of a grandma. You can be the wonderful fun grandma that they love while still telling them who's boss, ya know?"

Judy nodded. "You're right. It's time for me to take back my boss duties," she said with a giggle.

* * *

Around nine that night, Dave and Margaret walked along Hughes Street, just as Shannon and Ernesto had told them. It was dark and chilly out, and aside from a car passing now and then, all they heard were the sounds of an owl off in the distance. Some of the Victorian houses were lit up, probably with families inside, and others were pitch-black aside from the glow the moon casted upon them. When Shannon and Ernesto came around the corner, they immediately spotted Margaret and Dave.

"There you are. I'm so glad you guys came," Shannon said with giddiness.

Dave nodded. "Well, it's a nice night for a walk. It's quite stunning seeing so many houses lit up at night, but then you have these pitch-black ones. Maybe they're seasonal?"

Ernesto looked down the street. "Yeah, maybe. Or maybe they aren't lived in at all. Abandoned, almost."

Shannon pointed at a bright-blue house with sharp peaks at the top. "That one. That's the one."

Margaret shifted her eyes. "The one? What exactly are we going to see?"

Ernesto walked towards the house. "Just follow us. We don't want to say anything. Let's see if you notice."

Margaret and Dave looked at each other, shrugged, and followed behind them.

Once at the blue house that looked to not have anyone inside due to not a single light being on, they all stood on the sidewalk and stared at it.

Dave scanned the front of the house. "Well, it's a beautiful old Victorian. That's Cape May for you. I guess the fact that it looks empty might give it an eerie feeling."

"There's more. Follow us to the side of the house," Ernesto said as he discreetly opened the front gate and quietly tiptoed to the left side yard.

They all stood there, when Shannon looked up and gasped. "He's there, Ernesto. He's there!"

Margaret and Dave, bewildered by what was happening, squinted their eyes to see what they saw.

"Who's there?" Margaret asked as she looked up.

Ernesto and Shannon had already run back out to the side-walk, clutching onto each other.

Dave scratched his head and stared up at the attic window, not seeing a thing, when a cat began purring at his ankles and rubbing against his legs. "Oh, hey there," Dave said as he kneeled down to pet it.

Margaret looked over at Ernesto and Shannon as they stood on the sidewalk, signaling for them to come back over. She took one last look up at the attic window, catching a glimpse of a man. A shadow almost.

"Dave, did you see that? I saw a man in that window," Margaret said, starting to feel her heart race.

Dave looked up at the window after petting the cat, and saw nothing, then glanced at Ernesto and Shannon. "There's nothing up there. I think you're imagining things."

Margaret took a deep breath, then squatted beside Dave to pet the cat, but it immediately ran behind the house and out of sight.

They walked back over to Ernesto and Shannon. "Did you see him? The man in the window? We've seen him twice now." The couple vibrated with excitement and terror.

Margaret nodded, feeling a chill run down her spine, while Dave simply shrugged. "No, but I did meet a friendly cat."

CHAPTER SEVEN

Donna stepped into one of her old high school classrooms, and nostalgia overcame all of her senses. She walked around the empty room, picked a desk and chair in the back and sat.

"This is so surreal," she said to herself.

When the bell buzzed, students flooded into the classroom, prompting her to get up and go sit behind the teacher's desk. She was the substitute teacher, after all. The school had been so desperate for subs that they sped up the background check and called her bright and early to work the next morning.

The bell buzzed again, and announcements came on followed by the Pledge of Allegiance. Donna looked around the room, waiting for everyone to stop talking. When they didn't, she finally spoke up.

"Hello, class! I'm your sub today, Ms. Blaston," Donna said loudly over the commotion.

Brendan, a male student with shaggy hair in his eyes raised his hand in the back. "Miss Neville never leaves any plans for the sub, just so you know."

Donna looked at her sub folder. Sure enough all the instructions said were: *Have them take out a book for class and read quietly.*

Donna gulped hard. Surely, there was *something* for them to do, but if those were the instructions, so be it.

"OK, class. Today you're going to take out a book—" Donna was interrupted mid-sentence by a female student who walked right up to her.

"Ms. Blaston, can I please go to the nurse? I need an ice pack for my shoulder," the girl said.

Donna nodded, wrote her a hall pass, then continued on. "As I was saying, you are to read a book quietly."

The class chuckled, knowing full well that meant a free period, so they pushed chairs into groups to talk to their friends. Donna slumped into the teacher's chair by the chalkboard, opened her purse, and glanced at her phone inside of it. There was a missed call from Dale.

That's when a penny flew at her head. She ducked as it narrowly missed her and hit the chalkboard with a loud bang.

Donna stood up. "OK, who did that?"

The class was quiet.

"Did anyone see who did that?" Donna asked again, growing more aggravated.

Brendan raised his hand again from the back. "I'm pretty sure it was Max over there. He's known for tormenting subs."

Max glared over at Brendan. "It wasn't me, Brendan. Maybe you should shut your mouth," he said as his gaggle of friends laughed.

Brendan rolled his eyes. "Yeah, sure. What about this penny you just threw at me?" he asked as he held up the bronze coin, then proceeded to drill Max right in the middle of the forehead with it.

Max's face turned bright red as rage whipped through him, causing him to stand up and flip his desk. He stalked towards Brendan, who got up and moved near Donna.

"Help me," Brendan muttered under his breath.

Donna ran to the classroom next door and asked the teacher for help. Ms. Fetty, a six-foot burly woman with short, cropped hair and bigger muscles than even Dale, followed her into the classroom. As soon as the class saw her, they ran to their seats and folded their hands.

"I hear you're giving your sub trouble. Is that so?" Ms. Fetty asked as she walked around the classroom staring each student in the eye.

Nobody said a word.

"Well, I've told her to come get me if she hears one peep out of any of you again, and guess what will happen then? You will all be eating your lunch with me instead of the lunchroom with your friends. Not only that, but you'll also do detention with me after school. Am I clear?" she said with a stern voice.

Donna thanked Ms. Fetty, then breathed a sigh of relief as the class took out their books and read in complete silence for the rest of the period.

At lunch, she went out to her car and ate the sandwich she'd brought while calling Dale.

"Hey, there," Dale said as noises from his restaurant sounded around him.

"Hey, Dale. Today is nuts," Donna said as she took a bite of her turkey and cheese sandwich.

"Oh, yeah? It's your first day subbing. Is it bad?" Dale asked concerned.

Donna laughed, then sighed. "Let's just say I had to call in another teacher to come in and save me today. These kids are off the wall. I don't remember it being like this when I was in high school. I don't know if this is for me, and not just the subbing, but the whole teacher career thing."

Dale nodded. "Give it some time. It's only your first day. Don't make any rash decisions based off your first day. Promise me that."

Donna took a sip of her water. "OK. Fine. I promise."

Dale cleared his throat. "Oh! Have you heard back about the house rental in Cape May Point?"

Donna shook her head. "I haven't. I can't stop checking my

phone either, waiting for that email or call to pop up from the realtor. I want that house so bad it hurts."

Dale smiled. "From the photos online, that place looks pretty sweet. Much nicer than my rental. Plus, you've got the beach *right there.*"

Donna took another bite of her sandwich. "I know. I know. Don't make me more anxious than I already am. I hope I get it. It would be a dream."

* * *

Bonnie, Jackie, and Irene stayed after-hours at the Seahorse to watch a movie in the basement's home theater instead of hurrying off.

Irene flopped into a recliner and pulled the side handle, sending her feet flying up on the foot rest. "Let's watching something good. A tearjerker, but also romantic ... and inspiring. How about *When Harry Met Sally?*"

Jackie fumbled through the large stack of DVDs. "I don't see that one here."

Bonnie sat in the chair next to Irene's and pulled a blanket over her, then grabbed the large bowl of hot popcorn she just microwaved. "What about *You've Got Mail?*"

Jackie scanned through the DVDs some more before finally stopping on one. "Well, that one *is* here," she said as she popped the disc in the DVD player, then hopped into her seat next to Bonnie with the remote.

"Can someone dim the lights? I'm much too cozy under here," Bonnie asked as she popped a handful of popcorn into her mouth.

Irene rolled her eyes and chuckled. "Anything for the princess."

Just as Irene dimmed the lights, voices came down the steps.

"What should we watch tonight? *Breakfast at Tiffany's*?" Kim asked.

Dolly shook her head. "No, I was thinking something more along the lines of a dark drama," she said as she flicked the lights on.

Bonnie, Jackie, and Irene all squinted from the brightness just as the movie started playing.

"What is going on here?" Dolly asked.

Jackie cleared her throat. "Well, we're finished with work, so we decided to stay and watch a movie together. Have you ever noticed that this space was made to look like a drive-in theater?" she said as she pointed to the starry black ceiling.

Kim smiled and nodded. "It's great isn't it?"

Dolly nudged her in the ribs. "Yes, we knew that. However, Kim and I usually come down here to watch a movie. This is our night to do it."

Irene patted the chair next to her. "Well, you're more than welcome to join us. We're about to watch *You've Got Mail*, about a small bookshop owner who—"

Dolly flipped her hand in the air. "I've seen that one a million times."

Kim flicked the lights back off, grabbed a blanket from the shelf and sat next to Irene, giddiness overcoming her. "Pass the popcorn, I'm ready!" Jackie handed her the popcorn bowl as Kim leaned back into the recliner.

Dolly stood with her arms crossed. "Well, OK, then *Kim*. I see how it is," she said as she stormed back up the basement steps.

Irene looked over at Kim with a confused face. "What was *that*?"

Kim shrugged. "She's just grumpy. Turn the volume up. I love the opening scene!"

* * *

The firepit crackled at Willow Creek Winery as Dave and Margaret warmed their hands over it in their Adirondack chairs. Margaret opened a plaid fleece blanket and wrapped it around her shoulders, then looked over the variety of colors lined up in the glasses of her wine flight. "They all look so good. I don't know which to try first."

Dave smiled, while taking a glass of red from his flight. "I'm trying this one here. I'm curious about the notes of melon it says it has."

Margaret opted for a glass of white, taking a long sip and letting it warm her body even more than the fire. "Wow. I really like this one," she said as she set the glass down to try another.

Dave looked around at the dark vineyard before them, lit by only the moon and the smattering of outdoor string lights behind them. "I wouldn't mind growing grapes someday."

"Dave …" Margaret caught herself thinking about the night prior while she stared into the fire.

"Yes, Margaret," he said as he took a sip of wine.

The bright embers of the fire crackled as Margaret's eyes remained fixated on it. "Do you think there really may have been a ghost man in that window at that house last night? I saw him. I swear, I did. Even Ernesto and Shannon saw him."

Dave smiled and tapped Margaret on the shoulder, jolting her from her focus on the fire. "I don't know. I've never been into supernatural stuff. Never believed it. Then again, who's to say someone wasn't home? Maybe they like to save on the electric and sit in the dark or light candles?"

Margaret nodded. "Well … that could be a possibility."

Dave gazed around the outside patio. When his eyes landed on Greg having wine with a woman, his stomach dropped. He quickly swigged his wine, then stood up. "Well, it's getting cold out. How about we head back to the B&B and see what's going on there."

Margaret rolled her eyes. "Going on there? There's nothing going on there. There hasn't been all week. Plus, I have half a flight to finish here, and I'm enjoying myself. Sit down, Dave. Please."

Dave hesitated, then moved his chair to block Margaret's view of Greg, but it was too late.

"Hold up. I see Greg! Is that Liz with him? I want to go over and say hi," Margaret said as she craned her neck to see.

Dave fumbled on his words. "Oh, really? I don't know, it doesn't look like them," he said, trying to divert her attention.

Margaret stood and narrowed her eyes. "That's not Liz. Who is that?"

Dave sat quietly staring into the fire, not sure what to do.

"Katie? That's Katie. Why is he having wine with Katherine Duffield's assistant?"

Dave's stomach was tied in a complete knot by this point, and he quickly decided to discreetly text Greg.

Margaret and I are here at Willow Creek. She has spotted you. Get out now.

Greg glanced at his phone, then said a few words to Katie, and they both paid and hurried out of there through a back exit.

Margaret turned her head to watch them leave. "Where are they going? What's going on?"

Dave had to think up something to say quick. "I'm pretty sure it might be business related. Some kind of collaboration with Heirloom ... I also think it might be surprise for Liz."

Margaret took her last swig of wine, shifting her eyes, not sure what to make of the whole weird situation. "Well, I guess we can go now like you wanted. I'm done my wine."

Dave nodded, paid the bill, and they walked back to his truck, heading back to the B&B for the night.

They walked up the front steps of the Black Horse Inn and turned the key to the front door, stepping inside to an unsurprisingly pitch-black foyer.

Dave walked inside first, and using his phone's flashlight, led the way for them up the stairs.

Margaret stopped on the first step and turned around, looking into the dark abyss of the living room. "Wait. Did you hear that?" she asked with a whisper.

"Hear what?" Dave whispered back, looking in the same direction she was.

Bang!

"That," she said with widened eyes.

"Should we inspect?" Dave asked, up for a little exploring.

Margaret shook her head. "I don't think so … maybe it's better if we get to our room."

Dave shone his flashlight down the steps. "I'm going to go take a look. You coming with?"

Margaret stared up at the dark stairwell in front of her. "Well, I guess I should. I don't like being alone here."

They headed into the dark living room as Dave shone his cell's flashlight around the darkness. "I don't see anything."

Margaret latched onto his arm, as they headed into the dining room, still trying to be very quiet. "Dave. What's that door in the dining room go to?"

Dave shrugged. "The kitchen maybe?"

Margaret shook her head. "I think the kitchen is that way," she said as she pointed off to the right.

Just then, a woman's voice said, "Can I help you?"

Margaret gasped as Dave shined his light to see who it was. Behind them, Anne stood in the dark, watching them.

"We were trying to see what the loud noise was …" Margaret said as she stumbled on her words.

The flashlight still illuminated Anne's face as she glanced to the door in the dining room. "That needn't concern you. I'm sure it's just … the pipes."

Dave chuckled. "The pipes, yeah. These old homes make all sorts of noises. It makes sense. Come on, Margaret. Let's go back up to our room."

Margaret took one last glance around the room, and when she looked back at Anne, she was gone.

CHAPTER EIGHT

Liz finished staining the floors while still holding a bit of a silent grudge against Greg. She'd just completed the last corner of the living room, then stepped back to take a look, admiring her efforts.

As soon as Greg opened the sliding glass door into the kitchen, the dogs barreled inside. "Marley, Max! No!" Greg yelled after them.

It was too late. The dogs were much too excited to see Liz and tromped across the newly stained floor to get to her.

Liz screamed. "Oh my gosh! My floor. It has paw prints all over it. I have to completely redo this now."

Greg hollered at the dogs, "Marley and Max! Over here, now. You're going back outside, and then you're getting your feet deep cleaned." He ushered them back out into the yard, closing the slider behind them.

Liz stood in shock as Greg came back into the house. "Liz, I'm so sorry. I tried to block them, but they pushed the door open as I was coming in."

Liz tried to compose herself. Between her extensive home projects and Greg's secret little rendezvous, she was about to lose it. She pulled off her bandana, letting her hair fall to her shoulders, then quickly grabbed her purse and car keys off the counter. "I need to get out of here."

Greg widened his eyes. "Where are you going? Do you want me to fix what the dogs did on the floor?"

Liz flicked her hand in the air. "Do want you want. I just need to … leave."

Liz hopped into her car, turned up the fast-paced radio song to the max volume, and peeled out of the driveway, leaving a plume of dust in the air behind her. Five minutes later, she pulled into the Cape May Point Trails parking lot, and practically leapt out of the car. Speed walking helped her release all the pent-up energy and stress. About a half a mile in, she spotted a bench and fell onto it. She looked around at the beautiful trail, thinking about everything that had happened in the past week. Unbidden, tears ran down her face.

Liz wiped the moisture off her cheeks with the back of her sleeve. "Why are you crying, Liz? Stop," she said to herself. Mustering a deep breath, she took a few beats, then nodded at a couple walking by holding hands. "There must be a good reason Greg can't tell me why he's hanging out with some mystery woman, right?" she muttered out loud.

Having nearly composed herself, she was about ready to stand up when a gorgeous-enough-to-be-a-model man in his late twenties jogged up to her, pulling his earbuds out. "Hey. Mind if I join you for a minute? My shoelace is untied," he said as he pointed down to his bright-red sneaker.

Liz scooted over. "Sure. Have at it," she said as she looked away to wipe one last tear out of her eye.

The man tied his shoe then looked over at Liz. "You're beautiful. You know that?"

Liz was taken aback. Nobody had ever outright said that to her. It made her both happy and uncomfortable. "Oh, wow. Thank you … I guess?"

The man chuckled and stood up, before glancing at her

wedding ring. "Married. I bet he's one lucky man," he said as he jogged away.

After he was out of sight, a wide smile appeared on Liz's face. The guy wasn't being creepy. He was just giving a genuine compliment, and upon noticing her wedding ring, did the respectful thing and didn't go on any further. For a fleeting moment, she forgot about all of her stress and everything going on with Greg.

* * *

Margaret pedaled the rented electric bike and felt panic set in. "Whoa. How do I turn the settings down?" she yelled back to Dave, who was behind her riding happily along. They were headed down Sunset Boulevard, and Margaret wasn't sure if being on a bike with motor assistance made her feel more or less in control.

Dave yelled back over to her. "Look at your settings. Your settings!"

Margaret zipped down the road while trying to search for the settings. "I don't see them," she yelled back, feeling a bit frustrated.

Dave stared ahead at Margaret, watching her examine her bike while riding it. "Don't you remember what the guy at the rental place showed us?"

Margaret rolled her eyes. "I forgot it! I don't know!"

Dave chuckled. "Pull over up there at the honey shop on the right."

Margaret cruised her bike into the driveway and put the kickstand down, and Dave did the same next to her.

Dave looked over her bike. "Well, everything looks good, but I see the issue. You can choose how much motor assistance you want. You have it set at throttle mode, which means the bike is going to move without pedaling. Is that what you wanted?"

Margaret laughed. "Not really. I think I'd like to use some muscle with pedaling. I do need the exercise, after all."

Dave made an adjustment on the bike. "There, I switched you to pedal assist. Now you can pedal and still get some motor power with it. You ready to head back out?"

Margaret looked over at the Cape May Honey Farm shop. "I actually could use some local honey. Did you want to go in with me really quick?"

Dave shrugged. "Sure. Why not."

They walked into the honey shop, and Margaret was immediately drawn to some seasonal honey varieties. "Oh, wow. They have Pumpkin Blossom Honey," Margaret said as she held it up for Dave to see. "It says it has notes of caramel and toffee."

Dave nodded. "Let's get it. I bet that would be good in some hot tea this autumn."

Margaret smiled, and reached over to grab a basket in the corner, then plopped in the pumpkin honey.

"Growing up, some family friends of ours had a honey farm. Do you know how something like pumpkin blossom honey is made?" Dave asked as he browsed around the store.

Margaret shrugged. "Well, not really. How?"

Dave pointed to a little pumpkin decoration amidst the honeys. "It's nectar collected from bees who pollinated the big yellow blossoms on pumpkin plants. The flavor and color changes by what kind of plant blossom they pollinate. Fascinating, isn't it?"

Margaret nodded. "That's crazy. I never knew that. How do they know what the bee pollinated, though?"

Dave scratched his head. "From what I remember, the honeybee pollinates a two- to three-mile radius from their hive. So, when you're making a variety of honey, like pumpkin blossom, you place the hive in a spot where there's an abundance of a specific flowering crop in that radius. In this case, it was pumpkin crops."

Margaret's mouth opened. "What an interesting piece of information that I never knew."

Dave smiled and his eyes widened as he reached up to grab something called Winter White Honey. He handed the jar to Margaret. "Says it tastes like snowflakes on your tongue. Maybe we need a jar of honey for every season?"

Margaret laughed. "I think these two are enough for now. We'll come back again. I can't wait for the strawberry honey when strawberries are back in season next year. It's divine."

They paid and put their goodies in the baskets on the bikes before heading back out on Sunset Boulevard, this time with Margaret feeling much more comfortable and in control on her bike.

* * *

Chris and Sarah were standing in line for gelato at Cione Gelato with Sam, who was busy staring through the glass at all the delectable flavors. Sarah walked up next to Sam and deliberated with him. "What flavor do you think you want?"

Sam smiled and pointed. "The strawberry. What about you?"

Sarah sighed, then took one last glance at the case. "I want them all, really, but that tiramisu is standing out to me."

Chris put his arms around both of them while he leaned over and looked through the glass case. "And I'll take something with chocolate."

After ordering, they headed outside and found a little area to sit and eat. Sam took a heaping bite of his gelato, leaving some of it behind on his nose.

Sarah laughed. "You got a little something there, Sam," she said motioning to his nose.

Sam quickly wiped it off with his napkin, not sure whether to feel embarrassed or laugh.

Chris looked over at Sarah, then nodded, and glanced at Sam. "So, Sam. Mind if we have a little talk with you?"

Sam stared at his gelato, starting to feel like he may be in trouble. "OK, I guess."

"Well, I don't know how to ask this in a roundabout way, so I'm just going to come right out with it. What are your thoughts on your mother's boyfriend? Rick, is it?" Chris asked while taking a bite of his gelato.

Sam sighed, took a bite, then stared at his feet. "I don't know."

Sarah moved her seat right next to Sam, so their legs were touching. "You can tell us. We want to know the honest truth, whether it's good or bad."

Sam looked off into the distance, while setting his cup of gelato down. "Well, I don't like him. There, I said it."

Chris nodded. "OK, well we just want to get to the bottom of it. Is there any particular reason, or do you not like not having Mom to yourself?"

Sam looked at Chris and rolled his eyes. "Mom to myself? Give me a break. No, I just don't like him. He acts like the nicest guy in the world when Mom's in the room, and as soon as she leaves, it's like he turns into a different person. A mean one."

Sarah widened her eyes and stared at Chris, then looked back at Sam. "Mean how? Like strict mean? Like how you thought I was mean when I was worried about where you went the other night at the corn maze?"

Sam shook his head. "Nothing like you, Sarah. No, he says mean things when Mom's not around. He brags about his perfect kids, and tells me what I should do to be more like them. He tells me I look wimpy and should lift a weight or two. Stuff like that. When he's not doing that, he ignores me … like I'm not even there."

Chris stood up abruptly, his face red with anger. "Well, it

looks like I need to have a discussion with your mom. I'm not one bit happy about this."

Sarah nodded. "I agree. I would call her tonight."

They headed back home, got Sam situated for TV time before bed, and Chris and Sarah walked into the bedroom with the phone and shut the door.

Chris dialed his ex-wife Roberta's number.

"Hello, Chris. Everything OK?" Roberta asked.

"Um … sort of. Are you alone?" Chris asked.

Roberta paused. "Yes, why?"

"We found out some upsetting news tonight," Chris said.

"Oh no. What happened?" Roberta asked, panic rising in her voice.

Chris sighed. "Oh, nothing like that. Sam is fine. It's Rick I'm calling about. Sam doesn't like him …."

Roberta paused, then laughed. "You're calling about Rick? My boyfriend? And you're telling me Sam doesn't like him? I'm sure he's jealous. He's not used to another man being around since we got divorced. He'll get over it. Rick is a great guy."

Chris rolled his eyes while glancing at Sarah. "That's the thing, Roberta. What he told us—"

Roberta cut him off. "Look, Chris. I appreciate your concern, but there's nothing to be worried about, and I'm actually late to pick my mother up. Have a nice night."

Chris hung up, put his head into his hands, then looked up at Sarah. "That went absolutely nowhere. She doesn't want to hear it."

Sarah shook her head, remembering everything she went through with her stepmother, and a sinking feeling settled in her stomach.

* * *

Donna called Dale as she hopped into the car. "Dale! I got the house!! I got the house!" she yelled at the top of her lungs, excitement flooding out of her.

"You're kidding!" Dale said as he walked out of work, throwing his chef apron over his shoulder. "Did you get the keys?"

Donna jingled the keys in her hand. "Got them right here. You done with work?"

"I am. Just walked out after locking up for the night. Can I come over and see it?" Dale asked as he got into his car.

"Meet me over there. I'm heading over after I pack a few items to bring," Donna said as she hung up and started driving.

An hour and a half later, they both pulled up to Donna's little yellow beach house rental at the same time. Donna got out first, waved at Dale, then put the key into the lock for the first time, and opened the door. "Come on into *my* place, Dale," Donna said with a wide, giddy grin.

Dale's eyes lit up as he walked inside, taking notice of the open floor plan boasting a roomy living area and kitchen featuring a large butcher block counter on the island. He walked right up to the oven and opened it. "Not bad. Not bad. I could definitely whip up some good meals here."

Donna put her arm through his, walking him over to the bedroom. She opened the beach-facing window. "Stand right there, where the bed will go," she said while pointing to the middle of the room.

Dale walked to the middle of the room and stopped. "OK, now what?"

Donna looked out the window. "Well, it's not much of a beach view with all the trees blocking it, but the beach is on the other side of them. Let's close our eyes and see if we can hear it," she said as she stood next to him.

As the quietness settled in, suddenly a wave crashed off in the distance and Donna's eyes popped open. "Did you hear it?"

Dale laughed. "I did. You can hear the ocean."

Donna threw her arms around Dale and leaned her head back while laughing out of pure happiness. "I can hear the ocean from my bed, Dale. It's literally a dream come true. I've always wanted to fall asleep to the actual sound of an ocean, and not some recording."

Dale gave her a kiss on the forehead. "I'm so happy for you."

CHAPTER NINE

Early the next morning, Dave and Margaret finally decided to try breakfast at the inn. Margaret sat on the bed and bent down to tie her shoe while Dave buttoned his plaid flannel. "We still haven't seen anyone else here. It's so peculiar. We're probably going to be the only ones down there. Maybe we should just go to Mad Batter," Margaret said as she stood up.

Dave sniffed the air. "I don't know. Whatever they're cooking down there smells good. I think it's bacon."

Margaret shrugged, opened the door to the hallway and stepped out. "Alright, you ready?"

Dave walked out, leading the way down the stairs towards the dining area.

Margaret stopped him on the last stair. "Wait. Do you hear that?"

Dave chuckled. "What are you hearing now, Margaret?"

Margaret's eyes widened as she listened longer. "People. I hear actual people."

They walked into the dining room to see a long, gorgeous vintage dining table full of couples talking and eating.

Anne walked in holding an egg casserole dish, and set it

down on the hutch with the rest of the beautifully displayed breakfast buffet items. "Oh, you're joining us today finally?"

Margaret stumbled on what to say. "Oh, we like to sleep in. Taking advantage of not having kids here."

Dave nodded. "But this sure looks great. I'm starving."

Anne pointed to the two seats at the other end of the table. "Those seats are for you. There are drinks on the other side of the room. Help yourselves."

Dave grabbed the two plates from their place settings and handed one to Margaret. "Well, everything smells wonderful."

Margaret put two pieces of pumpkin cream-cheese-stuffed French toast onto her plate while Dave scooped some of the fluffy egg casserole onto his dish and topped it off with four large pieces of praline bacon. They sat down next to each other, across from another couple, and Margaret glanced up to see the strange old woman in the next room, staring straight at her from a chair in the corner.

Margaret nudged Dave. "Do you mind if we switch seats?"

Dave shrugged, not really understanding why, but happy to oblige. "Sure."

They switched, and Margaret took a sigh of relief upon realizing the couple now blocked the staring woman.

"Hi. I'm Noel and this is Dan," the woman said across from them. "We haven't seen you two at breakfast before. Just get in?"

Dave chuckled as he sipped his orange juice. "Nice to meet you. I'm Dave, and this is Margaret," he said while glancing at Margaret. "We like to sleep in mostly, and we have many favorite breakfast spots in Cape May that we were excited to get to, but now that I'm eating this, I'm really regretting not coming sooner," he said and then bit into the sweet and savory bacon.

Margaret took a taste of her French toast and widened her eyes. "Have you tried this French toast? I'm going to have to look up this recipe. It's incredible."

Dan displayed his empty plate. "I'm about to get some more. It was that good. Anyone want anything while I'm up?"

Everyone shook their head and said, "No, thanks."

Margaret then glanced at Noel. "You know. We've been here for a week now and have not seen one person. We were told the place was booked, so we've been quite puzzled, honestly."

Dan sat back down with his plate, just as Noel answered. "I told my husband the same exact thing. And why is it always dark after-hours? We can never see when we get in from a late dinner."

Dave nodded. "Right? Same here."

Margaret craned her head to see if the old woman was still in the other room, and sure enough, as soon as Margaret saw her, they locked eyes. Jerking back out of sight, she said, "There's something off about this place. I can't put my finger on it."

Noel widened her eyes. "I'm right there with you, Margaret. Did we check into the most haunted place in Cape May or something?"

Dave nearly choked on his drink as he started to laugh. "I don't know about that. These houses and inns are flat-out old. They make weird noises, they creak, they even have a different smell."

Dan took another bite of his French toast. "He's right. It's part of the charm."

Margaret and Noel glanced at each other, signaling that they thought there was more to it than just age and charm.

* * *

"OK, does everyone have a drink and popcorn?" Judy happily asked as she reclined back into the comfy movie theater chair.

Bob held his soda up on the other side of Judy. "Got mine."

Harper and Abby nodded at Judy as the lights dimmed and the previews started. Abby took a handful of popcorn, eyes glued to the screen, and tried to stuff it all into her mouth.

When popcorn kernels landed on Harper's lap, she said, "Hey!" while throwing a handful of popcorn at Abby.

Abby grew red with anger. "Why did you do that?"

Harper crossed her arms. "You did it first."

"I did not," Abby said as she flung popcorn at Harper. "But now I'm getting back at you for doing it to me."

Judy sat up in her chair as the movie started to play. "How about you two eat the popcorn instead of throwing it."

Abby's bottom lip trembled. "Well, tell Harper to stop throwing popcorn, then. She started it."

A person a couple rows away shushed them.

Judy whispered while leaning towards the girls, "Can't you two be nice to each other? We're here to watch a movie."

Harper glanced down in the dark at the popcorn on her lap that Abby had flung at her, picked it up, and tossed it back at her. "You can have your popcorn back."

Abby's temper boiled like a tea kettle ready to explode with steam. She screamed at the highest pitch possible in the dark movie theater then proceeded to run out the doors into the hallway.

Judy glanced at Bob. "Stay here with Harp. I'm going to go talk to her."

Abby sat on the rug against a new movie poster hysterically crying. "Go away," she said as Judy approached.

Judy sighed. "Abby, what's going on? Talk to me."

Abby turned her back to Judy and faced the wall. "I don't want to talk. I just want to go home."

Judy put her hand on Abby's shoulder. "How about we go back into the movie and you sit on the other side of Grandpa, away from Harper?"

Abby crossed her arms. "I'm not moving."

Judy thought about what Liz had said about being a grandmother figure more so than a friend with her grandchildren. Setting rules and boundaries would be a good thing.

She put her hand under Abby's arm. "Come on. We're going back in."

"No," Abby said, not budging.

At this point, Judy was rapidly swinging from frustrated to full-blown angry. She was tired of not being listened to, especially while going out of her way to do nice things for her grandchildren. She raised her voice three octaves. "At the count of three, if you don't get up, we're going back home, and you will do homework for the rest of the night. Do you hear me?"

Abby's eyes widened. Never had she heard her grandmother speak like that. "What?" she asked with surprise.

Judy glared at her. "I'm not messing around, Abby."

Abby slowly stood and walked with Judy back into the movie theater, all the while wondering what exactly just happened. Once in their seats, with Abby next to Bob this time, Bob touch Judy's hand. "It went well, I assume?"

Judy smirked at Bob. "I finally put my foot down is what happened. Prepare for the new Grandma Judy."

Bob chuckled, while squeezing Judy's hand, then focused back on the screen.

* * *

Sarah said goodbye to Chris as he headed out to finish some work at the dock, then walked to the kitchen table to do some bookkeeping for Monarch Coffeehouse. Sliding her reading glasses on, she opened her laptop, scanning the spreadsheet of expenses she'd made. A few minutes later, she abruptly slammed the laptop shut and leaned back in her chair. She couldn't stop thinking about what Sam told them or how badly Chris's conversation went with Roberta.

She walked to the fridge and ran her finger down the handwritten call list that Chris had put up for Sam in case of an emergency. She stopped at Roberta, pulled out her phone, and started dialing the number, but then stopped before the last digit.

"I shouldn't do this. Am I overstepping? We've barely met. I think I waved to her from the car when we picked Sam up. That was it," Sarah said out loud as she paced around the downstairs. Resolved, she sighed, then pulled out her phone again. This time she hit the last number before holding the phone to her ear.

It rang four times before Roberta picked up. "Hello?"

"Roberta?"

"Yes?" Roberta asked starting to feel concerned that this unknown caller was another telemarketer.

"It's Sarah … Chris's girlfriend."

Roberta was a silent for a moment. "Oh. Why are you calling? Is everything OK?"

Sarah gulped hard, trying to figure out how to go about this conversation. "I felt compelled to follow up with you about Chris's phone call last night."

Roberta sighed. "This again? Really? Do you two just not want me to be happy? Chris can find love again, but I can't?"

Sarah stammered on her words. "No. That's not the case *at all*. I don't believe Chris got a chance to explain to you our concerns about what Sam said."

Roberta bit her lip. "OK, well then, shoot. I'm sure it's all a big misunderstanding as he's a really great guy. You should see him with his kids."

Sarah took a deep breath. "Yeah, about that … Sam hasn't been himself lately, so we asked him about it together. Turns out, Rick has been not so nice to him. Do you know that once you leave the room, Rick acts like a completely different person to Sam?"

Roberta chuckled. "That's not Rick. He's nothing but loving and accepting of Sam. Maybe Sam is jealous?"

Sarah shook her head. "Hmm, well then, explain this: You left the room and he told Sam that he needs to be more like *his* kids. Then, he called your son a wimp and told him to start lifting weights. Also, he's gotten down on Sam about his facial features. He's putting self-doubt and worthlessness into your son's mind. Don't you see a difference in Sam?"

Roberta was silent. "My gosh. No, I don't see it. Is this true?"

Sarah nodded. "It is, and apparently Rick knows not to do it in front of you. He's been tormenting and ridiculing Sam behind your back. You can take this information and do what you will with it, but I really hope Sam no longer has to deal with it. You should see how sad he's been lately. Chris and I are very upset."

Roberta got choked up. "I feel like a horrible mother. Had you not called, who knows how long this would have gone on for since I dismissed everything Chris tried to tell me."

Sarah took a deep breath. "Please do something about this. I can't bear to think of Sam enduring it any longer. I was once in his shoes, and it took years of therapy to get through."

Roberta wiped a tear from her eye, and called Sam over from his bedroom. "Sam, come here please."

Sarah listened on the other end, while Sam walked over.

"Give me a hug," Roberta said with tears in her eyes.

"Why?" Sam asked befuddled.

"Just do it," Roberta said as she opened her one arm.

"OK, fine," Sam said as he wrapped his arms around her.

Roberta started crying. "Sam, I love you, you know that? Do you know how special and amazing you are?"

Sam looked up at her. "Why are you crying?"

Roberta smiled and wiped the tears out of her eyes. "I heard about Rick. We won't be seeing him again. I promise you that."

Tears welled up in Sam's eyes as he hugged her tighter.

And Sarah was still on the line and had started crying along with Roberta.

"You still there?" she asked Sarah after Sam went back to his room.

Sarah cleared her throat and wiped some tears out of her eyes. "I'm still here. Always here for you guys."

* * *

Dave pulled his truck into the parking lot of Nauti Spirits, the local distillery in town, while Margaret gawked at the large piece of land full of rows of dried cornstalks, a little farm stand, and plenty of outdoor seating.

Dave hopped out of the truck and walked around to open Margaret's door.

Margaret smiled as she held Dave's hand while stepping out. "My oh my. Who says chivalry is dead?"

Dave blushed and kissed her hand as they walked. "You ready for a cocktail?"

"Am I!" Margaret said as she held his hand through the entrance of the building.

They got their hands stamped, then turned around to see all the tables filled with people playing board games.

Dave turned to the woman who'd stamped their hands, and before he could say anything, the woman smiled. "Yep, that's right. It's game night tonight. Go find a game and grab a drink. Enjoy yourselves."

Margaret chuckled watching Dave's eyes widen in excitement. "Oh, what game should we play?" he asked as they walked towards the bar area.

Margaret strolled over and picked up Jenga. "How about this one?"

Dave sighed and smiled. "I don't know. That one makes me so anxious for when it falls, but I think I spy something even better," he said as he eyed another game.

Margaret laughed. "Scrabble? Really? You can't get enough of this game all of a sudden."

Dave shrugged. "Hey. I like what I like. How about you hang here at the table, and I'll go get us some drinks?"

Margaret nodded and proceeded to set the game up on the table.

Five minutes later Dave walked back with two colorful gorgeous cocktails made with fresh ingredients. Margaret took a sip and smiled. "Amazing, thank you, Dave. But you know I'm going to kick your butt at this game, right?"

Dave rubbed his hands together. "We shall see about that. My family is known for having throw-down Scrabble matches at every get-together."

Margaret pointed to herself. "Mine too!"

Dave laughed. "Well, I guess we've got ourselves a healthy competition then, huh?"

An hour later, Dave used the last of his letter tiles to make a forty-point word.

Margaret looked at her two remaining letters and sighed. "I've got nothing. You win."

Dave took the final sip of his drink. "Wanna play again? I'm just getting started."

Margaret shook her head. "I'm one and done. How about we walk around the property? It's a beautiful piece of land they've got here," she said while pointing out the windows.

Once outside, there were people sitting around firepits, and the air was crisp and cool, exactly as expected for a late-October night. They walked onto the grass, and Dave pointed up at the sky. "Look at those stars. I bet that bright one is a planet."

Margaret sighed and smiled. "I miss Harper and Abby."

Dave put his arms around Margaret. "Me too. I can't believe I get to be their stepdad. I know we can't turn back time, but I sure wish we'd met sooner."

CHAPTER TEN

Eighties music blared as Liz painted the dining room walls, the next project on the list after she'd finished up the living room.

She rolled the taupe paint up and down the wall with the paint roller, then stopped to scratch her nose with the side of her arm. She glanced into the living room, taking notice of the nice job Greg had done fixing the stain on the floor where the dogs had mucked it all up the other day. A warm feeling crept into her heart—until she remembered all of the secrets he wouldn't explain to her.

She walked across the room, cranked the music up, and went back to painting, this time finishing the wall in record time from all of the adrenaline that pumped through her veins.

Knock. Knock.

Liz furrowed her brow. Who would be knocking on her door? They lived on a farm at the end of a long gravel drive-way. Hearing knocks on the door, unless expecting company, wasn't exactly the norm.

She walked to the door, peaked through the window first, then opened it slightly.

"Hi, there. I have a delivery for Liz. Is that you?" the young man asked as he held his clipboard.

Liz shifted her eyes. "For me? I didn't order anything."

The man looked back at his clipboard. "Well, it appears I have the right address. Stay there, I'll be right back with it."

Liz folded her arms while she watched the delivery driver open the back of the van and walk inside of it. He stepped out with three bouquets of red roses. Altogether, the arrangement of the three dozen roses were so big, she couldn't see the driver's face as he walked back to the door and handed them over.

"Well, have a nice day, ma'am," the man said as he hopped back into his van and headed off to the next delivery.

Liz fumbled with the roses while bringing them into the house, then placed them on the counter as she looked for vases in the cabinets.

After filling the third vase with water and placing the last bouquet of roses perfectly inside of it, Liz buried her face into them, inhaling their scent. "Who sent these?" she asked the empty room.

Just as she was about to throw the florist's wrappings into the garbage, a small card mixed with it caught her eye.

Three dozen red roses for the light of my life.
I would not want to share this wonderful life with anybody but you.
You are my heart and soul. Always remember that.
Love, Greg

Liz read the card once over and slumped into a stool by the roses. She smiled, letting her heart feel full from the letter and roses, and with some hesitation, she started to let herself be patient with Greg. He'd said to trust him about the situation with Katie, and she was going to try, even if it was incredibly hard.

* * *

Over at the high school, Donna's second day substitute teaching was even worse than the last time she'd been there. During her lunch break, she went to the teacher's lounge, found an empty table, took a seat, and pulled out her sandwich. As she took a bite, she stared at the wall, deep in thought.

Suddenly, the door to the teacher's lounge swung open, and in walked Ms. Fetty with her loud teacher squad. "Donna, how are you making out today?" Ms. Fetty asked as she popped her meal in the microwave.

Donna sighed as she took a sip of her sparkling water. "It's going good," she said unconvincingly.

Ms. Fetty pulled her meal out of the microwave, stirred it up, then brought it to Donna's table and took a seat. "For real this time. Tell me how it's *really* going."

Donna dropped her sandwich and took a deep breath. "I'm subbing for a math teacher today, and let's just say this class was taking full advantage of me. Running around the room, loudly playing music, inviting their friends in from the hallway. As much as I tried to talk over them, no one cared or listened. The funny part is, I thought I wanted to be a teacher, you know, as a career, but I'm starting to think I'm not cut out for this."

Ms. Fetty let out a loud laugh, startling Donna. "Sorry. I had to get that out. Now, all of us in here went through that at first. However, you have to understand that a substitute teacher is usually treated differently than staff teachers by the students. They see it as a free pass to act up. There's a sweet spot where you learn to be a teacher who isn't to be reckoned with, while also being kind. You can't let them walk all over you."

Donna nodded. "You're right, I guess. Well, wish me luck," she said as she stood up just as the bell rang. Donna arrived back to her classroom just as all the students filed in. Instead of sitting at their seats, they perched on top of the desks and in corners on the floor, talking loudly.

"Can I have a hall pass?" a female student asked as Donna got situated with the lesson plans the teacher left.

Donna squinted her eyes. "For what?"

The student thought for a moment. "Well, I have to return this book to the library."

Donna looked at her seating chart. "Allison, is it?

"That's me!" Allison said.

"Great, have a seat," Donna said with a plastered smile.

Allison shifted her eyes, confused by what just happened.

The class was loud with everyone talking and laughing, paying no mind to Donna. So she loudly slapped the white-board with a ruler, then flicked the lights off and on.

Everyone stopped talking and looked over at her.

"Great. Now that I have your attention, we're going to do a math lesson. I know you think it's a free period, but it is indeed not. Get out your math books," Donna said as she stood at the front of the classroom and turned the overhead projector on.

"Yeah, I'm not doing any math today," a male student in the back said as he put his feet up on the chair in the front of him and started up a video—at full volume, no less—on his phone.

Donna nodded and smiled. "Peter, is it? Do you want to be written up? Or maybe you prefer a trip to the principal's office. If you don't open your math book and pay attention, you will win a chance at either."

Peter sat up, looked around the room at everyone else, now sitting in their seats and getting their books out, then he sighed and took his out.

Donna inhaled a deep breath, finally feeling satisfied that she could handle this on her own.

* * *

Kim and Dolly were leaving their shift at the Seahorse just as Irene, Jackie, and Bonnie pulled into the driveway.

Dolly grasped Kim's arm. "I just remembered I forgot to clean one room," she said as she ran back up the porch steps into the inn.

"Do you need help?" Kim called as Dolly fled.

Dolly flicked her hand, so Kim took it as a sign that she didn't need help. She said her hellos to Bonnie, Irene, and Jackie, then got in her car and drove out of the driveway.

Inside, Dolly ran up the staircase. As she got to the hallway, she tripped on the rug and flew headfirst into the wall, then landed unceremoniously on her side.

"Oooooohhh! Owww!" Dolly moaned as she held her head. "Kim?" she nearly wept from the hallway, feeling dizzy, lightheaded, and nauseous.

"No, it's just us. Kim left," Jackie said she hung her coat on the coat rack.

Dolly moaned again.

"Are you OK?" Irene yelled up the stairs.

"Not really, but I've got it. I'll be OK. No need to come up here," Dolly said as she tried to get back on her feet.

Thump! The house shook as Dolly fell back on her butt from the dizziness. Jackie, Irene, and Bonnie all rushed up the stairs, one after the other, to Dolly's side, where Irene immediately knelt.

"Get me the bag of frozen peas in the freezer and two throw pillows," Irene directed Jackie and Bonnie.

"I'm fine. I just took a little tumble on that rug," Dolly said as she leaned against the wall, holding her head. Jackie and Bonnie were back in a flash, handing the frozen peas to Dolly to put on her head, while propping her back and arm with the pillows.

Irene crouched down even further to examine Dolly's head. "It looks like you're going to have a good bruise there. Did you hurt anything else?"

Dolly shook her head, but then pointed to her arm. "Maybe a little rug burn."

Bonnie sat next to Dolly against the wall. "Do you feel like you may have a concussion? Did you want one of us to take you to urgent care to get checked out?"

Dolly sighed but noted the pain and dizziness had begun to subside. "Honestly, I'm starting to feel better already. I didn't hit the wall too hard. I think I'm mostly shaken up. I'll still call my doctor today just in case, though," she said as they ladies helped her to stand.

"How about you rest in a chair in the living room for a little bit before your drive home," Irene suggested, still looking at Dolly with concern.

Dolly flicked her hand in the air. "I'm fine, plus I never cleaned this last room. Let me get that done really quick, then I'll head home."

Jackie lightly touched Dolly's arm. "We've got it, Dolly. Don't worry about that."

Dolly nodded, unsure how to respond to these women who usually only annoyed her, but who had been so loving to her in a time of weakness. "Well, OK, then. Thank you. I do appreciate it." She descended the stairs, feeling more than a little embarrassed by how she'd been acting towards them all week.

* * *

Around 7:30 p.m., Dave and Margaret were at the B&B getting dolled up for dinner. Margaret spun around in her long-sleeve floor-length autumn-colored dress. "Do you like?"

Dave finished buttoning a cuff and glanced over. "Wowza. That's all I've got to say."

Margaret smiled, then kneeled down in front of the little mirror on the table to apply her red lipstick. "Well, I'm ready when you are. Shall we walk over?"

Dave looked at Margaret's heels. "Well, it's only a couple of blocks away, but that's up to you."

Margaret glanced at her shoes. "Oh, I wore these during a

long night out in Paris. If they can handle cobblestone streets, they can handle Cape May sidewalks."

Dave chuckled as he tucked his shirt in, and combed his hair back. "Well, off we go, then."

Walking hand in hand, they eventually got to the Washington Inn, which was stunning to look at all lit up at night. Dave glanced at the string lights hanging over the outdoor tables. "It's a beautiful evening, so I called and asked for outdoor seating. I hope that's OK."

Margaret squeezed his hand. "I'm glad you did. Not sure how much longer we'll be able to sit outside and eat as the weather gets colder."

They got to their table, and a waiter greeted them with a bottle of champagne.

"I'm Jim. I'll be taking care of you tonight," he said as he poured the champagne into the two champagne flutes on the table. "Can I start you with any other drinks?"

Margaret widened her eyes at Dave, delightfully surprised by the champagne. "I'll take a water with lemon for now."

"Same," Dave said as he took her hand from across the table.

The waiter left, and Dave smiled while holding his glass up. "I ordered this as a surprise. A celebration of our love. Cheers to you and me."

Margaret clinked her glass against his and took a sip of the bubbly drink before glancing at the menu. "Everything here looks divine. I want it all."

After ordering, their food eventually came to the table.

"Here is the branzino for you, ma'am, and the crab cakes for you, sir," the waiter said as he set the beautifully plated dishes in front of them.

Margaret took another sip of her champagne before cutting into her fish dinner. Her eyes closed as she took her first tasty bite. "This is excellent. How is yours, Dave?"

Dave had nearly finished one of the two crab cakes.

"Really good, but I'm starving, so they're going fast," he said with a chuckle.

Dave paused and glanced at Margaret. "So, everything is really all set for our dinner with family and friends in two days?"

Margaret put her fork down. "I think so. Everyone said they could come, surprisingly. It's going to be a full house. I'm so excited," she said with a wink.

Dave nodded. "Well, good. It'll be great to see everyone, and I sort of have a little surprise for you."

Margaret rubbed her chin and squinted at Dave. "A surprise? Really? How about you give me a clue."

Dave smiled. "Nope. You'll find out soon enough."

* * *

After dinner, Margaret and Dave happily strolled through the tree-lined streets dotted with Victorian houses. The smell of a distant wood-burning stove filled the air, and the fallen leaves all over the sidewalk crunched underneath their feet as they walked.

Pow! Pow! Pow!

Margaret whipped her head towards a large oak tree behind them. "What was that?"

Dave scanned the area, spotting two squirrels chasing each other up a tree. "Those are acorns falling."

Margaret walked over to examine, noticing acorns everywhere. She bent down when one fell from the tree and clunked her on the head. "Ow!"

Dave gave a hearty chuckle. "You OK?" He asked as he rubbed her head.

"I'm fine. I guess I was hoping it was something spooky again," Margaret said as she continued down the sidewalk. "But who knows, maybe all of this spooky stuff all week was all in my imagination."

Dave shrugged, then pointed down the road. "Let's head over towards the beach. There's somewhere I want to take you."

They arrived to Beach Avenue and stopped in front of Hotel Macomber, gazing at a large mermaid statue.

"Interesting. Never noticed this before," Margaret said as she walked over to the statue.

Dave pointed behind the garden. "Did you see the love lock garden there?"

Margaret held her hand over her heart as she walked to the chains holding locks with names and dates engraved. "I love this."

Dave casually pulled out a lock from his pocket. "I had one made for us."

Margaret's jaw dropped as she took the lock from Dave. She smiled, looking at the date. "Our wedding date. You put it on here. I love this, Dave."

Dave put his arm around Margaret and smiled. "Pick a spot to lock it, and then we'll throw away the key, locking our love forever."

Margaret looked at a nearby lock. "Katherine and William. They sound nice. We'll lock our love next to theirs," she said, pushing the lock closed before giving Dave a kiss.

"It's getting a little chilly out. Would you like my jacket?" Dave asked as they walked back down the street.

Margaret felt a shiver run down her spine. "OK, but I think I'm ready to go back to the Black Horse for the night. Let's head back that way."

Dave gave her his jacket and put his arm around her back as they made their way through the beautiful (but somewhat spooky) old streets again. Upon returning, they walked through the front door of the dark inn, using their phone's flashlights to guide their way again.

Margaret started up the stairs first, each step creaking loudly underneath their feet until finally they got to their room.

"Why is the hallway pitch-black? They have guests who need to see, after all."

Dave shrugged his shoulders. "Beats me."

Once they got into their room, they both immediately changed out of their dress clothes and into comfortable pajamas. Margaret pulled the covers back off the bed and hopped in. "How is it midnight already?" she asked as she looked at the clock beside the bed.

Dave slipped in beside her while yawning. "Well, it was a two-hour meal, and then we walked for a while," he said as he sank into the pillow, his eyes closing swiftly.

Margaret turned to him. "Dave, do you want to stay up and light a fire or something?"

Dave answered by loudly snoring. Margaret rolled her eyes, turned the light out next to the bed, then pulled the covers up to her chin. There was a gap in the curtains that allowed the bright moon to shine right into their room, illuminating it. She closed her eyes and tried to sleep.

Thunk!

Margaret sat straight up in bed, not believing what she just heard.

Thunk!

But there it was again.

"Dave, wake up," Margaret said as she nudged him.

Dave stopped snoring for a moment, but then started up again. This time even louder.

Bang!

Margaret stared up at the ceiling, growing scared and curious at the same time.

She reached to the nightstand for her cell phone. "Great. It's dead," she muttered.

Slipping out of bed, she walked to the dresser, lit the candle in the brass candlestick holder and carried it to the door. Slowly opening it, she let herself stick her head out and search the hallway. It was still pitch-black, and it had appeared everyone was settled for the night.

She held the candle out as she walked slowly down the hall towards the rear of the inn; opposite of the staircase they'd use for coming and going every day. She and Dave hadn't explored that part of the inn yet, and as she moved closer, she could see a door was open at the very end.

"Should I look? What if the people in that room forgot to close their door?" she thought to herself. As she glanced hesitantly into the darkened room, holding her candle up, a hand came down on her shoulder.

"Ahhhhh!" Margaret screamed at the top of her lungs.

"Margaret, what are you doing?" Dave asked, half-asleep in flannel pants and slippers.

"Dave, you nearly gave me a heart attack," Margaret said, annoyed.

Dave shook his head. "Try waking up in a strange dark room without the person you came with."

Margaret sighed. "Let's get back to bed. I was trying to see where the bangs were coming from."

Dave rubbed his eyes. "There were more bangs?"

Margaret nodded as they walked into their room, shutting the door behind them. She blew the candle out, and placed it on the dresser before noticing something out of the corner of her eye.

"Dave … don't move," she whispered. "Look behind you."

Dave slowly turned, and standing there, beside the window, was a ghostly silhouette wearing Victorian clothing.

"Do you see that?" Margaret asked, barely moving as she spoke.

Dave stared harder. "I do, looks like a shadow."

Margaret watched as it vanished into the air, then her and Dave both sat on the bed.

"Dave, I'm not crazy, right? We both saw that? There was a

man right there by the window. I don't know if I'm going to be able to sleep tonight."

Dave didn't respond, so Margaret turned the light on. Dave was laying flat on his back, snoring heavily as though he hadn't just seen a Victorian ghost.

She left the light on for the rest of the night, staring at the spot by the window.

CHAPTER ELEVEN

It was Friday, Margaret and Dave's last day of vacation at the B&B, and Dave awoke to find Margaret's side of the bed empty. He got showered and dressed, and walked downstairs, wondering where she went off to.

"Margaret?" he asked as people ate breakfast in the other room.

"I'm out here," her voice rang from the front porch.

Dave opened the door to find Margaret sipping on coffee, while reading a book in the rocking chair.

"Up early today, eh?" Dave asked as he sat next to her.

Margaret sighed. "I couldn't sleep very well … unlike you. How did you fall asleep so quickly after seeing something so frightening?"

Dave chuckled. "It just looked like a shadow to me, I wasn't scared. You didn't sleep at all?"

Margaret shook her head. "After you fell asleep, the bathroom door opened on its own. Then, the light by the bed flickered and the old radio in the corner came on for a split second. I heard a few more loud bangs above the bed, like before. I tried to wake you, but you were out like a light."

Dave's eyes widened. "Well, try harder to wake me next

time. I'd protect you against the scary ghosts," he said with a snicker.

Margaret looked at him and rolled her eyes, knowing he still didn't believe it.

Dave nudged her playfully and smiled. "What are you reading?"

Margaret turned the cover towards Dave. "This *Spooky Cape May Stories* book. I completely forgot about it after I bought it. I guess because it got tucked back into my suitcase. There is something I want to show you in this, though," she said as she handed the open book to him.

Dave took it from her and glanced at the open page. "The Black Horse Inn is in here. I remember you said that while we were at The Ugly Mug …."

Margaret bit her lip. "Read the second paragraph."

Dave read aloud. "'The Black Horse Inn is considered to be the most haunted inn in Cape May. According to the previous owners, Edith and Harry, they experienced paranormal activity on a constant basis. When having work done to the house, they had workers leave unexpectedly, never coming back to finish the job. They kept a log book of anything reported by guests over the forty years they ran the inn. By all accounts, the most haunted room reported was the honeymoon suite. In that room, many guests claim to have seen a male in Victorian clothing.'"

Margaret stared at Dave with widened eyes, waiting for his reaction. "Well …?"

Dave scratched his chin. "So, you're telling me that you just now read this story? You hadn't read it before now?"

Margaret shook her head. "Not until this morning. Is it a coincidence that we saw the same exact thing that all of these other people did? I think not. And according to this book, we are staying not only in the most haunted inn in Cape May, but also the most haunted *room*. We're in the honeymoon suite, Dave."

Dave handed the book back to Margaret as a chill went down his spine. "Well then, I guess I'm glad we're finding this out on our last night here … even if I don't believe in all of this."

Margaret chuckled as Anne stepped outside, her long silver hair blowing in the breeze.

"Hi, there. Will you two be eating breakfast? Wanted to check before we put everything away," Anne asked as her eyes landed on the ghost stories book.

Margaret looked at Dave and shrugged. "I think we're OK. We might head out in a bit and grab brunch somewhere."

Anne tried to form a smile. "Well, tonight we're having desserts and wine in the living room. I'm just starting it back up today. Why don't you two come join us around eight."

"Sounds nice," Dave said as he nodded at Anne.

* * *

In Cape May Point, it was Donna's official move-in day. Dale helped unload everything out of the moving truck. It only required the two of them, as Donna didn't have much since her ex-husband, Adam, kept possession of most of their furniture in California after the divorce.

After unloading the truck, Donna looked around the empty house. "Wow, I've got some shopping to do. I need a couch, TV, dining table and chairs—you name it. I have a bed and dresser, but that's about it," she said as she motioned to the bedroom.

Dale rubbed his stomach. "You hungry? Because I am. How about I go grab us a pizza, and we can sit on the living room floor and eat it?"

Donna laughed. "Sounds great. I'll organize a little while you're out."

Thirty minutes later, Dale arrived with a piping-hot

margherita pizza. "Donna?" he asked as he walked around the house looking for her.

"Outside," Donna yelled from the backyard.

Dale found Donna in the back corner of the yard, sitting on a chair left behind by the owner.

"Dale! Bring the pizza over here. You've got to see this."

Dale walked over to Donna, then stopped in disbelief. There was a large enough gap in the thick trees to see the beach and ocean on the other side."

Donna jumped out of her seat. "Can you believe this? I can actually see the ocean from my yard. I mean, I knew it was right on the other side of the trees all along, but I never thought I'd be able to see it from here."

Dale walked towards the gap holding the pizza and shimmied sideways through the trees onto the beach, then turned towards Donna. "Looks like you have your own personal beach access too. Wanna sit on your new beach and eat some pizza?"

Donna ran over to him, feeling more excited than ever. "You bet I do."

They sat on the cool sand with nobody else around, enjoying the pie and serenity of it all.

Donna gave a long, happy sigh after she finished her slice, then stared out towards the ocean. "Did I mention I had a really great day substitute teaching yesterday? Well, at least the second half of the day. I think I'm getting the hang of this teaching stuff," she said with a pause. "My gosh, it feels like everything in my life is falling into place. I can't believe how lucky I am to live here."

Dale nodded and put his arm around her. "And you'll live even closer to my place in Cape May, which is an added bonus. Though, seeing this house is making me happy my lease is only month-to-month, I may have to look around for something in this neighborhood."

Donna looked straight at Dale "Yeah, I've been trying to figure out how to talk to you about that. How do you feel about moving in with me? I kind of insinuated that someone else would be living with me on the lease … you know, just in case."

Dale smiled from ear to ear, which was enough of an answer for Donna.

* * *

Sarah walked out onto the street after her shift at the Monarch Coffeehouse, when a familiar truck pulled up next to her as she was about to get into her car.

"Well, hello there, stranger," Chris said as Sam enthusiastically waved from the back seat.

"Hey guys! What are you doing here? Couldn't wait to see me?" Sarah joked.

"We're going to pick out pumpkins to carve. Come with us!" Sam yelled.

Chris smiled. "What do you say? A little autumn fun, just the three of us?"

Sarah opened her car door. "Perfect. I'll meet you over there. Dawson's Farm, I'm assuming?"

Chris nodded as he shifted the truck into reverse. "Looking forward to it."

Twenty minutes later, they were all walking around the little farm with rows and rows of pumpkins and gourds in all colors and sizes. Sarah held up a bumpy red pumpkin. "How about this one? It's pretty unique," she asked Sam.

Sam scrunched his nose. "I'll pass on that one."

Sarah and Chris looked at each other and started cracking up.

"Can I go on the hay bales over there where the kids are?" Sam asked.

Chris flicked his hand in the air. "Go on over."

Sarah walked over to a table of blue pumpkins and picked one up to examine it. "Oh!" she exclaimed when someone wrapped their arms around her from behind.

"It's me, silly," Chris said as he hugged her tight.

Sarah turned around with a smile. "That was unexpected."

Chris shrugged. "You're amazing. I needed to hug you in that moment."

Sarah laughed, facing the table display again. "OK, mister. Help me pick out a pumpkin."

Chris didn't move. "Roberta told me you called her the other day."

Sarah's eyes widened as she turned to look at Chris. "Really? What did she say?"

"She told me to thank you. She had no idea what her boyfriend was putting Sam through. She broke up with him, thankfully, and she talked with Sam, and he told her everything —even more than he told us. Roberta and I had a nice long chat, and I'm glad we're communicating better about what's best for Sam. And it's all because of you, Sarah," Chris said as he cupped her face in his hands, then planted a kiss on her lips.

In the midst of running back to the pumpkins, Sam caught sight of them kissing, and instead of interrupting, he found some nearby pumpkins to look at. He had more of a fondness towards Sarah now. It may have taken time, but he was glad she was in his life.

* * *

By early evening, Dolly was at home finishing baking up a storm on her day off.

She picked up her phone and called Kim.

"Hi, Dolly," Kim said happily as she answered.

Dolly pulled a pumpkin cranberry nut bread out of the oven. "Kim! So glad you answered. Are you doing anything?"

Kim looked down at the purring cat on her lap and then at her husband snoring on the couch with the remotes on his chest. "Not really. What's up?"

Dolly started icing her carrot cake cupcakes with one hand.

"Well, you remember what I told you happened yesterday at the Seahorse, right? How I fell?"

Kim nodded. "Yes, how are you feeling?"

Dolly shook head. "Never mind that. I'm fine. I never told you how Irene, Bonnie, and Jackie came to my rescue. They were so sweet to me, such lovely ladies."

Kim rolled her eyes. "I know. They are nice people. You were too stubborn to notice over the past week."

Dolly sighed. "I know. I know. I want to go over tonight and apologize, but I can't do it alone. Will you come with me?"

Kim glanced at the slippers on her feet. "Fine. Let me get my shoes on."

An hour later, they pulled up to the Seahorse in Dolly's car. Walking up the steps to the B&B with full arms, Dolly managed to pull the door open with her foot and held it wide for Kim to move through.

"Oh, let me get those for you," Bonnie said as she hurried over and took some of the baked goods from Dolly.

Irene walked down the stairs. "What are you two doing here? It's your day off."

Dolly sighed as they all walked into the kitchen. "I know. I thought I'd make you guys some treats for the fun of it."

Jackie walked in from the dining room, and took the pumpkin bread from Kim and placed it on the kitchen table. "This looks lovely."

Kim cleared her throat. "Dolly, tell them why you *really* made the treats."

Everyone quietly waited to hear what Dolly had to say.

Dolly looked around the room. "I'm sorry. That's why. I was a stubborn old bat when I met you three, and I apologize. I was wrong about you ladies. Thank you for helping me yesterday after I fell."

Irene nodded. "We appreciate it, Dolly, but you didn't have to go through all this. It was too kind of you. Would you like to stay and have a bite with us? We have a little time before we have to start preparing wine-and-cheese hour."

Before anyone answered, Kim took a seat at the kitchen table and sliced the pumpkin bread. "You bet we're staying to eat."

* * *

Since it was their last night, Margaret wanted to make sure they made it back to the Black Horse Inn by eight for the wine and dessert than Anne had mentioned. As she and Dave walked back from dinner, Margaret caught a glimpse of the inn under the moonlight.

"Do you really think anyone is going to be downstairs? It's always so dark whenever we get back from being out at night," Margaret asked as they walked up the steps to the front door.

Dave sighed. "Your guess is as good as mine. We shall see."

There in the foyer and off in the living room and dining room, instead of complete darkness, were about fifteen large candelabras, burning brightly with candles. Margaret's eyes widened as she walked towards the many guests standing and talking while drinking wine in the living room. In the middle of the living room was a lit fireplace, and on either side of the fireplace were ceiling-high bookshelves full of old books.

Dave walked around the room in astonishment noticing little things like the ornate purple velvet couch that he'd never noticed before. He wandered around some more before he was startled by the old woman in the chair, staring directly at him from the corner.

Anne walked in the room wearing a long black gown that made her silver hair pop against it. "You've come to join us tonight. I'm so glad. There is wine and cheese in the dining room. Help yourself."

Margaret nodded. "It's lovely, Anne. It's nice to not see it so … dark at night."

Anne looked around the room. "Well, we like to save on electric when we can," she said with a chuckle. She looked over at the old woman in the corner. "Where are my manners. Have you met my mother, Ethel, yet?"

Margaret shook her head, then looked towards the old woman. "Is that who that is? We were wondering."

Dave nodded in agreement as he walked over to pour two glasses of wine.

Anne sighed. "Yes, she's staying here with me for the time being. She can't live on her own anymore, bless her heart. She takes turns staying with all seven of her children. I think tomorrow is when my brother comes to pick her up."

Dave handed a glass of white to Margaret, then glanced out the front window when he spotted a stopped trolley full of people gawking at the inn.

Anne followed Dave's gaze. "Ah, yes. The trolley ghost tours are going on tonight."

Dave squinted his eyes. "Is your inn on the ghost tour?"

Anne nodded. "It is. Didn't you know it was haunted?"

Margaret glanced at Dave. "We soon figured that out, well at least I did."

Anne looked around the room. "Yeah, I noticed your *Spooky Cape May Stories* book this morning. I'm sure you saw our inn is in there. My husband and I weren't too happy about that."

Dave cocked his head. "Why is that?"

Anne sighed as she walked over and tidied up the wine and cheese. "Well, we were afraid that it would scare people off from staying here."

Margaret shook her head. "I actually think it would help business. A lot of people love these sorts of things. They even search them out. When did the book come out?"

Anne paused in thought. "Recently, actually. That's when they started putting us on one of the haunted trolley tour routes. But now that you mention it, we did book up rather quickly for the next few weeks. Maybe you're right."

Dave walked over to make a cheese plate and he was reminded of the mysterious door in the dining room. "Anne, we've been meaning to ask you what's behind this door?"

Anne laughed. "That's where my mother stays. Sometimes she wanders around the house and I have to go get her, though. You may have noticed that the one night."

"And what about the bangs we hear?" Margaret asked.

Anne shrugged. "That I can't explain. Some say it's the man who passed away here in the early 1900s. He was sick and would always bang on the wall by the bed when he needed something from the nurse. That's something that's not in the book, but maybe we'll let the writer know now."

Margaret sighed, and a chill went down her spine as she took a sip of her wine. "Everything makes sense now."

Dave put his arm around Margaret, then looked back over at Anne. "Does your mom happen to like playing Scrabble?"

Margaret glanced at Dave and playfully nudged him. "You and this Scrabble."

Anne's eyes widened as she smiled. "She does, but I'm warning you, she always wins."

CHAPTER TWELVE

The next morning after checking out of the B&B, Margaret walked around the three long wooden farmhouse tables under the canopy of pine trees at the Pinetree Wildlife Refuge, neatly positioning the autumn napkins next to each place setting.

Dave was unfolding chairs and tucking them in under the table, when he stepped back and looked everything over. "Well, that about does it. Are you finished?"

Margaret nodded, while smiling. "I'm so glad the refuge let us host our family and friends here."

Dave glanced around the property, taking in the fresh pine scent he'd missed while they were on vacation. "Me too. Really, it was all Joan. She took care of securing it for us." He glanced at his watch. "We need to be getting back. We still haven't unpacked."

Margaret yawned. "You're right, and I want to take a little nap. I slept even worse at the Black Horse Inn last night after it was officially confirmed by Anne that it was haunted, especially being a couple days before Halloween—that makes it extra spooky somehow."

Dave's eyes widened. "Really? I slept like a baby."

Margaret shook her head. "Oh, I know you did. You slept right through everything again."

"What did I miss this time?" Dave asked.

Margaret tapped her chin as she looked up in thought. "Let's see. The man in the attic must have really needed the nurse last night because he banged at least ten times."

"I miss everything," Dave said with a laugh.

Margaret shook her head and playfully nudged Dave. "I thought you didn't believe in all that ghostly stuff?"

Dave shrugged. "Well, I may have been swayed just a little. Not gonna lie."

Margaret chuckled as they walked back to the truck together, hopped in, and took off for her house.

* * *

Around six that evening, when Margaret, Dave, Harper and Abby arrived to Pinetree Wildlife Refuge and were walking towards the tables, they could see everyone was there already, dressed up for the nice evening out.

Margaret smiled and nudged Dave as they headed over together, hand in hand. "Your parents are here, even your sister came from California. Oh, look there's my Aunt Linda and Uncle Mike, and all of my cousins."

Dave shook hands with everyone, and Margaret gave hugs as they said their hellos. Meanwhile, Harper and Abby had run over to be with their cousins.

Liz hurried over from the table where she'd been sitting with Donna, Dale, and Sarah. "Margaret, what on earth kind of dinner is this?"

Margaret furrowed her brow. "What do you mean?"

Liz pointed to the Edison bulbs hung by a line over the three long tables, then she pointed to the tables.

Margaret craned her neck to see. Her eyes widened as she stared at completely different tables than what they'd left that morning. There were huge autumn floral arrangements in the middle of the tables. Their modest place settings had been replaced with fine china, the plastic folding chairs that Dave had set up were replaced with old wooden vintage chairs of different styles, and next to the floral arrangements were enormous cheese, meat, and fruit charcuterie boards.

Liz watched as Margaret gawked at the table in disbelief. "Did you hire someone or something?"

Margaret shook her head as she grabbed Dave's arm. "Dave did you see *this*?"

Dave stopped talking with his brother to look over, when his mouth dropped open. "What in the world? Who did all of this?"

Everyone looked around at everyone else, trying to see if someone would fess up. Nobody did.

Chris broke the silence as he walked up to the group with a martini. He took a sip and nodded at Dave. "Great bar you've got over there. You guys really did this dinner up."

Dave scratched his head as he walked a little path behind the trees to a makeshift bar staffed with two bartenders mixing up fresh cocktails while a few of their family members stood in line waiting to order.

Dave walked up behind Margaret and handed her a glass of wine, then took a sip of his Manhattan. "Here you are, my lady," he said while Margaret glanced at the menus on the table. Their pasta meals and Caesar salads were now filet mignons, lobsters, crab cakes, and an assortment of other things.

Margaret took her glass of wine, and held up the new menu for Dave to see. "Somebody went all out. Did Joan do all of this?"

Dave shook his head. "I doubt it. She doesn't have this kind of money. Who could have possibly done all this?"

After another forty-five minutes of cocktails and talking, everyone took their seats at the tables. Conversations could be heard from all corners as servers came by to get their entree orders.

Dave clinked his glass and stood up, walking to the head of the table. He motioned for Margaret to join him. "We want to thank everyone for coming out. We wanted to find a way to get all the people we love together for a nice evening. This past year has been a whirlwind with jobs and life, and it's nice to stop, breathe, and take the time to be with those you love."

"Here! Here!" Dave's dad yelled from the back.

Margaret held her glass up for a toast, and everyone lifted their drinks.

Dave took a sip of his Manhattan, then glanced at Margaret. She nodded back at him. "Well, we do have something to announce, as well."

Everyone put their glasses down, waiting to hear what they were going to say.

"We had a long talk, and I guess you could say our engagement is off," Margaret said as she looked at everyone.

Everyone's eyes widened in disbelief as they looked at one another, not sure of what to say.

Dave cleared his throat. "I think what Margaret is trying to say is … the engagement is off because we're officially getting married tonight. Right here, with you all."

Everyone gasped in surprise, then clapped and cheered, while Harper and Abby ran to Margaret and Dave and gave them a big hug.

Margaret beamed. "While you all talk amongst yourselves, we're going to get changed to make this official."

Twenty minutes later, Margaret and Dave were back in their wedding attire. Margaret in an elegant off-white lace wedding gown, and Dave in a black tuxedo. They stood at the head of the table as Margaret's dad got up with them, standing beside them.

Suddenly, headlights could be seen coming up the driveway, causing everyone to stop and look over.

A stretch black limo pulled in, and out stepped Katherine Duffield, William Hansen, Dottie, and Vivian, and a few other celebrity friends of Katherine's.

Margaret gasped when she saw who it was as they approached, all of them wearing long shimmering gowns or tuxedos. Everyone else at the tables gasped along with her.

Katherine looked over at Margaret and Dave standing at the head of the table. "Oh no. Did we miss it? Katie said to be here at seven."

Margaret and Dave smiled. "You didn't miss a thing. We were just about to start."

Katherine gave a sigh of relief. "Oh, good. I hope you don't mind that I upgraded your wedding for you?"

Margaret laughed. "You did this? But how?"

Katherine glanced at William and smiled. "Dave asked Greg to get ahold of me. He thought it would be neat if we could possibly come to your wedding, since we became friends while we were filming in Cape May. It was then that I offered to take care of the wedding—unbeknownst to Dave or Margaret—and my assistant Katie took care of all the secret planning with Greg. And boy did the two of them get it done," she said as marveled at how beautiful everything looked.

Liz glanced at Greg. "Katie? Is that the *Katie* you were with?"

Greg nodded. "Yep. We were planning this wedding. I made a vow to Dave not to tell you about the wedding. Margaret wanted you in on the surprise. I guess I'm a good friend because keeping that secret nearly ruined my marriage," he said with a chuckle.

Liz smiled. "It looks like you had two secrets to keep. Dave's and Katherine's. I must say, I'm impressed." She planted a big kiss on Greg.

Katherine and the rest of her celebrity group took their seats as Margaret and Dave walked back to the head of the table, faced each other, and held hands.

Bob took out his notes as he stood before them. He had gotten ordained just for this special occasion.

Dave's eyes turned misty as he started his personalized vows. "Margaret, you are my everything. You're my best friend, the sun in my sky, the holder of my heart. I've never told you this, but when we first met here, working at this refuge, I couldn't take my eyes off you. Your beauty is like no other, and well, I tried to hide my adoration for you by never talking to you."

Everyone laughed.

Margaret laughed along with them, then piped in. "It's true. He barely talked to me. I thought he hated me."

Dave cleared his throat and continued on. "I love the way your freckles stand out on your nose. I love how you care for Harper and Abby. I love when you have dirt all over you from the garden, and I especially love how you love me. I can honestly say I never knew love until I met you. This past year and a half has been the happiest time of my life, and it's because of you. I can't imagine this life without you. So, Margaret, I vow to be your loving husband and that the four of us—Abby, Harper, you, and I—will be a loving family forever."

Margaret wiped the tears out of her eyes. "How do I even top that?" Everyone at the tables laughed as Margaret herself started to laugh between the tears.

Margaret composed herself, then looked deep into Dave's eyes. "We found each other during our lowest time here at the refuge, and for that, this place will always have a special place in my heart. I wouldn't want to marry you anywhere else. You have brought so much joy to my life, and Harper and Abby's lives. You're amazingly handsome, even if you don't know it, and my heart still flutters when you touch me as though it were the first time. I feel so lucky and blessed to be spending the rest of my life with you, and I vow to always to be there for you as your wife."

Dave and Margaret wiped tears out of their eyes as they

happily gazed at each other. They exchanged rings while Bob pronounced them man and wife.

Everyone stood up and clapped as Dave dipped Margaret for a romantic kiss. They turned to face everyone, then took their seats at the dinner table just as the servers came around with the meals.

Greg glanced over at Katherine and winked, then stood up and tapped his water glass with his fork. "Attention, everybody. Katherine has also graciously added a reception tent on the other side of the property. Music will be played without disrupting any of the wonderful resident animals that live here in the structures Dave built."

Margaret squealed with excitement as she looked to catch Katherine's eye. "Thank you," she mouthed to her.

Katherine looked over at William and back at Margaret. "No, thank you," she mouthed back.

Greg continued on. "There are multiple golf carts that we will be taking to the reception after dinner."

Everyone clapped as their gorgeous salads arrived chock-full of autumn vegetables like beets, carrots, and butternut squash mixed with kale and pomegranate seeds.

After dinner, they headed over to the reception on the golf carts. Margaret got in alongside Dave as he drove them down the sandy road towards the other side of the property. The wind whipped Margaret's hair around as she laughed and held onto her dress tightly, hoping it didn't blow up. They rounded the corner and saw a huge tent with firepits and couches along the outside of it. There was another bar with bartenders, and white string lights had been strung all throughout the wide-open grassy meadow.

Dave helped Margaret out of the golf cart as everyone else pulled up alongside them and headed towards the tent.

"Dave, can you believe all of this? It's like a fairy-tale wedding. It's absolutely stunning and perfect," Margaret said as her eyes lit up with happiness.

Dave leaned over and kissed Margaret as they stepped onto the large dance floor and a slow song began playing. "I think this is our song. How about a dance as husband and wife?"

Dave twirled Margaret, then pulled her close to him. She laid her head on his chest as they swayed to the music, taking notice that everyone was standing around watching them. Margaret motioned for their friends and family to come join them on the dance floor. One by one, each of the couples that they loved so dearly started slow dancing around them.

In that moment, Margaret gave a sigh of relief, knowing not only that her heart was in good hands with the man of her dreams, but that her life was so blessed with wonderful people, new and old.

EPILOGUE

It was Christmastime and Margaret, Dave, Harper and Abby were out at a Christmas tree farm one cold early-December evening looking for a tree.

"How are we feeling about this one?" Dave said as he stood next to an eight-foot spruce.

Margaret nodded. "Looks good to me. What do you think, girls?"

"I think it could possibly work. Though, maybe we need something bigger?" Harper asked. Abby nodded in agreement with Harper.

Margaret laughed. "Any bigger, and we'll have to cut a hole out in the ceiling. I think that tree will be perfect, Dave."

Dave got down on his knees and started sawing away. "Step back, everyone. I don't want the tree to fall on you."

Margaret put her arms around the girls' shoulders as she ushered them off to the side. Suddenly the tree fell, but right on top of Dave. From the ground, he stared through the needles at Margaret and the girls as they tried to hold in their laughter.

"I'm OK. Don't worry about lil' ole me," Dave said with a chuckle as he stood up and wiped his jacket off. They hauled the tree back to Dave's truck where he secured it with rope, and then headed over to the hot chocolate stand where many families were hanging out.

Margaret's phone rang, so she said, "Dave, can you get the girls some hot chocolate? I'll be right over. I'm going to take this call."

Margaret answered her phone without looking. "Liz, I've been trying to call you all day. The Candlelight Christmas Tour is starting an hour early this year—"

"Hello?" the person on the other end said.

Margaret paused. "Liz?"

"No, this is Katherine."

"Oh, my gosh. I'm so sorry, Katherine. I thought you were my sister."

Katherine chuckled. "No problem at all."

Margaret smiled. "Katherine, I can't thank you enough for everything you did for our wedding. It was the most magical evening. You are such a kind and generous woman. Dave and I can't stop talking about how amazing everything was."

Katherine nodded. "You are more than welcome. It was the least I could do. Staying at the Seahorse really changed me for the better. Not only that, but it reunited William and me. I felt I owed it to you, but that's not why I'm calling."

"Oh?" Margaret asked surprised.

"Do you remember the movie we shot in Cape May? It was called *Dinner Under the Stars*."

"I do. How could I forget? How could the town forget?" she said with a chuckle.

Katherine smiled. "Well, that's great to hear because we're doing the movie premiere at The Cape May Movie Theater next May."

Margaret furrowed her brow. "The Cape May Movie Theater? That place hasn't been in business since I was a kid. Maybe thirty-some years ago. Are you sure you have the right place?"

Katherine took a sip of her wine. "Oh, I'm sure, alright. I just bought the old abandoned theater. I'm having it restored to its former glory. It should be done in time for the premiere. I guess you could say I fell in love with Cape May while falling in love in Cape May and wanted to do something for the community."

"That's wonderful, Katherine. I'm so happy to hear that," Margaret said as she glanced towards Dave and the girls drinking their hot cocoa.

"Well, you'll all be getting a personal invite to the premiere. And if you don't mind, I'm going to give my friend who's restoring the place your number. You, Liz, and Dave seem to know how to get an old building back up and running. Maybe you'll have some tips. We'll talk soon."

"That sounds great. Bye, Katherine," Margaret said as excitement took over her.

* * *

Pick up **Book 9** in the Cape May Series**, The Cape May Movie Theater,** to follow Margaret, Liz, the rest of the familiar bunch, and some new characters

Check out my store where you can get deals on my books at www.ClaudiaVance.com

ABOUT THE AUTHOR

Claudia Vance is a writer of women's fiction and clean romance. She writes feel good reads that take you to places you'd like to visit with characters you'd want to get to know.

She lives with her boyfriend and two cats in a charming small town in New Jersey, not too far from the beautiful beach town of Cape May. She worked behind the scenes on television shows and film sets for many years, and she's an avid gardener and nature lover.